Buried Treasures of Texas

Books in W.C. Jameson's
Buried Treasures series:

Buried Treasures of the American Southwest
Buried Treasures of the Ozarks
Buried Treasures of Texas
Buried Treasures of the Appalachians
Buried Treasures of the South
Buried Treasures of the Rocky Mountain West
Buried Treasures of California
Buried Treasures of the Pacific Northwest
Buried Treasures of the Atlantic Coast
Buried Treasures of New England
Buried Treasures of the Great Plains
Buried Treasures of the Mid-Atlantic States

Books on audio:
Buried Treasures of the Civil War
Outlaw Treasures

Buried Treasures of Texas

Legends of Outlaw Loot, Pirate Hoards, Buried Mines, Ingots in Lakes, and Santa Anna's Pack-Train Gold

W.C. Jameson

August House Publishers, Inc.
LITTLE ROCK

Published 1991 by August House, Inc.,
P.O. Box 3223, Little Rock, Arkansas, 72203,
501-372-5450.

Printed in the United States of America

10 9 8 7 6

LIBRARY OF CONGRESS CATALOGING-IN-PUBLICATION DATA

Jameson, W.C., 1942–
Buried Treasures of Texas : legends of outlaw loot, pirate hoards, buried mines, ingots in lakes, and Santa Anna's pack-train gold / W. C. Jameson — 1st ed.
p. cm.
Includes bibliographical references.
ISBN-13:978-0-87483-178-8 (acid-free paper)
ISBN-10: 0-87483-178-4 (acid-free paper)

1. Texas—History, Local. 2. Treasure-trove—Texas—Folklore.
3. Legends—Texas. I. Title.
F386.6.J36 1991
976.4—dc20 91-31771
CIP

Executive: Liz Parkhurst
Project editor: Judith Faust
Design director: Ted Parkhurst
Cover design: Wendell E. Hall
Typography: Lettergraphics, Little Rock

This book is printed on archival-quality paper which meets the guidelines for performance and durability of the Committee on Production Guidelines for Book Longevity of the Council on Library Resources.

AUGUST HOUSE, INC. PUBLISHERS LITTLE ROCK

For Marylee, my precious daughter

Contents

The Gulf Coast

East Texas Piney Woods

Introduction

Texas! The very name conjures images unlike those of any other state. These images, which have blended into the overall American culture and are recognized virtually the world over, include the pervasive figure of the Texas (hence, American) cowboy, the longhorns he herded, and the romance and struggle of the trail drive; outlaws the likes of Sam Bass and John Wesley Hardin on the rough and dangerous frontier; the frontier itself, that great, sometimes nearly impassable barrier to settlement and westward expansion; the "wild" Indian, the warring Comanches, Apaches, and Kiowas who aggressively defended their lands against Anglo encroachment and made settlement a dangerous undertaking.

Woven into, through, and around these colorful images are the many stories, tales, and legends that have sprung from the fertile and varied terrain of Texas and its diverse peoples: folktales such as those about Pecos Bill; fantastic stories of the deeds and exploits of the almost mythical Texas Rangers; the colorful adventures and daring of real-life characters like Bigfoot Wallace, Jean Laffite, and Charles Goodnight; and tales of ghosts and hauntings, of spirits, witches, and demons. Among the most enduring, powerful, and contagious of all were the tales of lost mines and buried treasures.

The many stories of lost treasure to come out of Texas are a product of the people and the land. The tales are not restricted to any one culture—they have been handed down from the Indians, the Spanish explorers who sought gold and silver, the early Mexican and German settlers who came to establish farms and ranches, the pirates who plied the waters of the Gulf Coast, the Southerners and the Appalachian backwoodsmen who migrated westward to find land and opportunity, and from many others. These diverse cultures evolved into a rich fabric of humanity which characterizes Texas today, and which, in so many ways, is a product of the varied Texas environment.

It is little wonder that the wide variety of adventurous souls who contributed to the settlement of the Lone Star State could also contribute so much to its folklore heritage.

ENVIRONMENT

In spite of the widely held image of Texas as a vast, barren, unbroken plain, the environments within the state's boundaries range from humid and marshy coastal lowlands near the Gulf to rugged, pine-forested mountain peaks stretching nearly nine thousand feet into the clear West Texas skies; from waterless high plains in the Panhandle to sere deserts in the West to dense, damp pine woods in East Texas; and from South Texas's brush-covered, rock-strewn gullies to the cavern-riddled limestone hill country of Central Texas to the black soil and cross timbers in the north of the state.

Variety? Most certainly. Texas may be able to claim more environmental variety within its boundaries than any other state in the union, a variety that means major differences in weather patterns, soil, vegetation, and wildlife from place to place.

CULTURE

The physical environments of Texas are no less varied than the many cultures that have resided in and or passed through the state, each of which has added some element to the cultural characteristics of this rich landscape.

The first residents of Texas were Native Americans. Though reputed to be fierce, warlike heathens preying on white settlers, the Indians of Texas were never particularly numerous and only practiced a way of life suited to survival in rugged, sometimes treacherous, environments. Apaches, Comanches, Kiowas, Wichitas, and others roamed the plains and mountains of West Texas, often following the vast herds of buffalo that foraged on the rich plains grasses. A few tribes of a more sedentary nature occupied portions of the East Texas forests and the Gulf Coast regions.

The first contact Indians had with whites occurred when Spanish explorers under the leadership of Francisco Vásquez de Coronado entered the region. On a mission from the King of Spain, Coronado had orders to find wealth and transport it back to the motherland to fill his country's coffers. Legend has it that while traveling throughout Texas, Coronado learned of rich gold and silver mines long operated by local Indians, and he and his soldiers and miners searched for and apparently found ore in great quantities. That the Spaniards mined gold and silver throughout much of Texas has been well documented, as has the fact that tons of bullion was shipped from the interior of the state to the coast and thence to Spain.

The years 1815 through 1836 were the initial period of Anglo settlement in Texas, and most of those who entered the region during this time were hardy backwoodsmen from the Appalachian province of the Upper South—mostly Kentucky, Tennessee, and North Carolina—and a smattering of settlers from Arkansas.

The first successful Anglo settlement came in the northeastern corner of the state while Texas was still under Spanish rule and became firmly fixed around 1820. The settlement was purely an accident, for the newcomers began farming the lands along the Red River valley under the mistaken belief they were actually in Arkansas!

During the next decade, Anglo settlement gained momentum with the help of the newly independent

Mexican government, which worked hard to attract newcomers to the province. In cooperation with the Mexican government, several people were given large land grants intended to convince farmers and ranchers to move into the interior. The Austin, DeWitt, and Robertson Colonies were the first, and population grew steadily in this southeastern part of Texas, consisting primarily of migrants from Arkansas, Kentucky, Missouri, and Tennessee. During this period of Mexican rule, Texas began to take on a cultural flavor reminiscent of the Upper South.

Beginning about 1830, German immigrants came to Texas in response to advertisements they saw in Europe. Lured by the promise of abundant and fertile land, the initial German migration was somewhat unorganized but resulted in a modest accumulation of settlers in an area between the lower reaches of the Brazos and Colorado Rivers. German colonization continued into the 1840s, eventually producing a "German Belt" across a portion of South–Central Texas.

Texas also attracted numbers of Czechs, Slavs, Poles, Wends, and Slovaks, some Scandinavians, and a few French and Irish Catholics.

Following Texas independence in 1836, the immigration of Anglos increased dramatically. More and more people from the Lower South (Alabama, Georgia, Louisiana, and Mississippi) were attracted to Texas as a result of the relaxation of Mexican laws against slavery. The Lower–South Anglos arrived in great numbers, accompanied by their slaves, and began to challenge the Upper–South Anglos for dominance. By the time of the Civil War, these two subcultures were localized in distinct parts of the state, separated by an imaginary line extending roughly from Texarkana to San Antonio.

From the Civil War to about 1880, migrants from both the Upper and Lower South continued to flood into Texas, and were accompanied by a small number of New Englanders.

During this time, blacks made up a significant portion of the growing Texas population. By the time of the Civil War, nearly one-third of Texas was black.

The roots of the Hispanic influence in Texas stretch back to the period of Spanish and Mexican colonization which lasted from 1680 to 1836. For the most part, the Spanish attempt at the colonization of Texas was a failure, due in part to the low esteem in which they held the region. While they did experience some successes in the mining of gold and silver, they essentially considered Texas to be little more than a buffer zone between Mexico and the encroachment of the British and French. Furthermore, the Spaniards continued to be frustrated by continued attacks from the area Indians, principally Apaches and Comanches.

After Spanish rule ended in 1821, the Mexican government fared little better at successfully colonizing the area. Scattered throughout Texas, however, were small pockets of Mexican farmers and ranchers who established viable settlements, many of which still exist today.

This incredible melting pot of people created the cultural diversity of the region and certainly provided for variation in the character of the landscape, for along with each cultural or ethnic group came its unique baggage which included specific religious preferences, dietary habits, language, agriculture, architecture, and of course its folkways, including storytelling traditions.

During pioneer days in early Texas, the chief source of entertainment was community gatherings at which music was played and elders took turns telling tales. Storytellers often related versions of historical and current events, sometimes mixed with local legend and folklore. These tales were presented dramatically and colorfully, and were sometimes used to interpret the history of the region and the people as it was known at the time. Many stories handed down in the oral tradition dealt with lost mines and buried treasures, for at the time, the Texas countryside fairly teemed with prospectors, miners, adventurers, and treasure hunters in search of gold and silver. Many tales had substantial documentation while others were of obscure origin, the facts long since lost or dimmed by time.

Among the first attempts to collect and preserve these wonderful tales of lost mines and buried treasures were the efforts of writer-folklorist J. Frank Dobie, a Texan whose articles and books inspired so many to undertake the search for lost and hidden wealth. Dobie's compilations of many of these tales were collected and published by the Texas Folklore Society. His most famous book, *Coronado's Children,* considered a classic in the genre, has introduced thousands to the world of buried-treasure folklore and has likely lured thousands more into the forests, fields, deserts, and coasts of Texas in search of buried treasure.

Like the children of Coronado Dobie wrote about, there are a legion of "Dobie's Children" who continue to explore, research, collect, and write about the stories of buried treasure associated with the state of Texas. This book, *Buried Treasures of Texas,* represents years of research and exploration in libraries and in the field, and is intended to pass on some of the most fascinating and provocative of the tales. The stories as presented here result from long search and research, countless hours in libraries around the country tracking down references and writings, interviews with knowledgeable individuals and prospectors, thousands of miles of travel and thousands of hours of investigation.

I and others have searched for many of the treasures in these stories. While in most cases, no treasure was found, enough leads and consistencies were encountered to be encouraging about the validity of the stories. In some few cases, treasure *was* actually found, but that is another book.

The stories in this book are ultimately the products of the people of Texas—their experiences, their adventures, their lust for exploration and wealth and good stories. These tales are a gift from them and from the geographic and cultural environments that spawned them. As such, they are indeed a treasure in every sense of the word.

The State of Texas

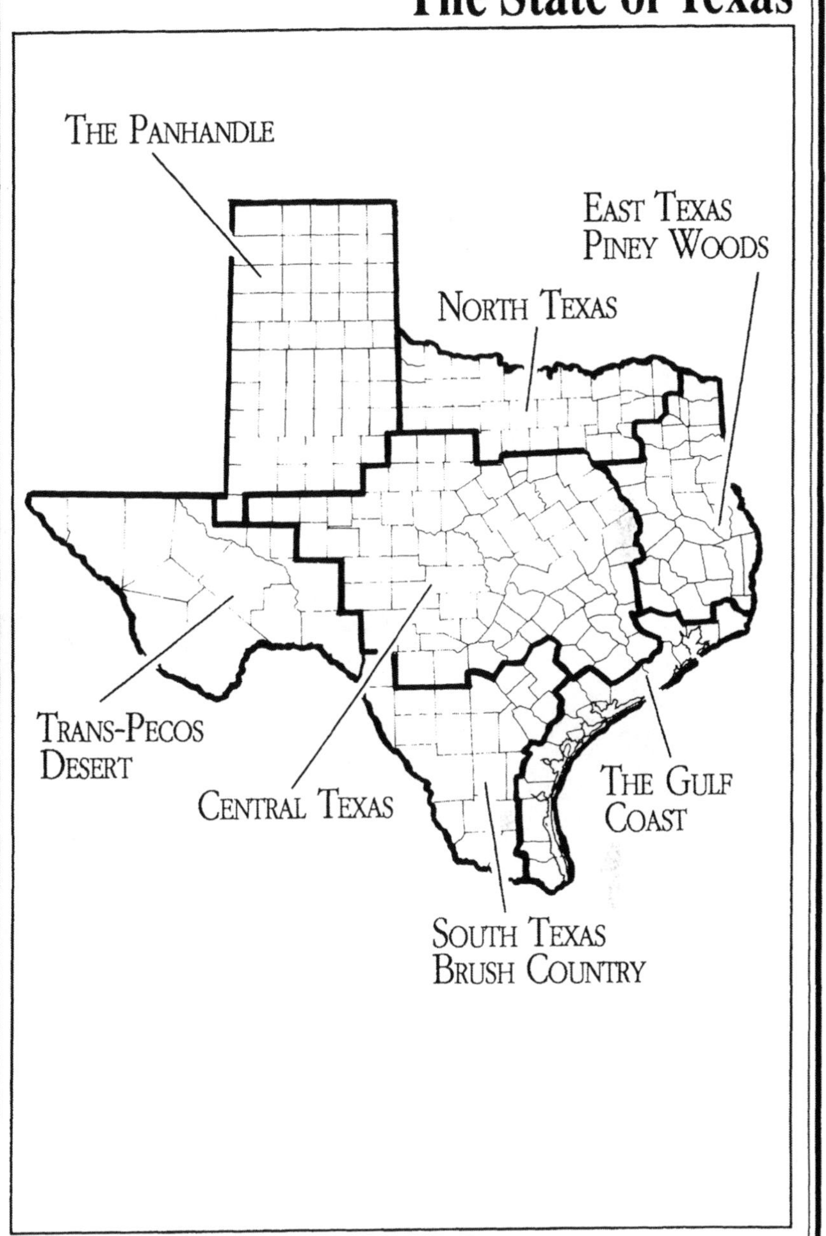

The Trans-Pecos Desert

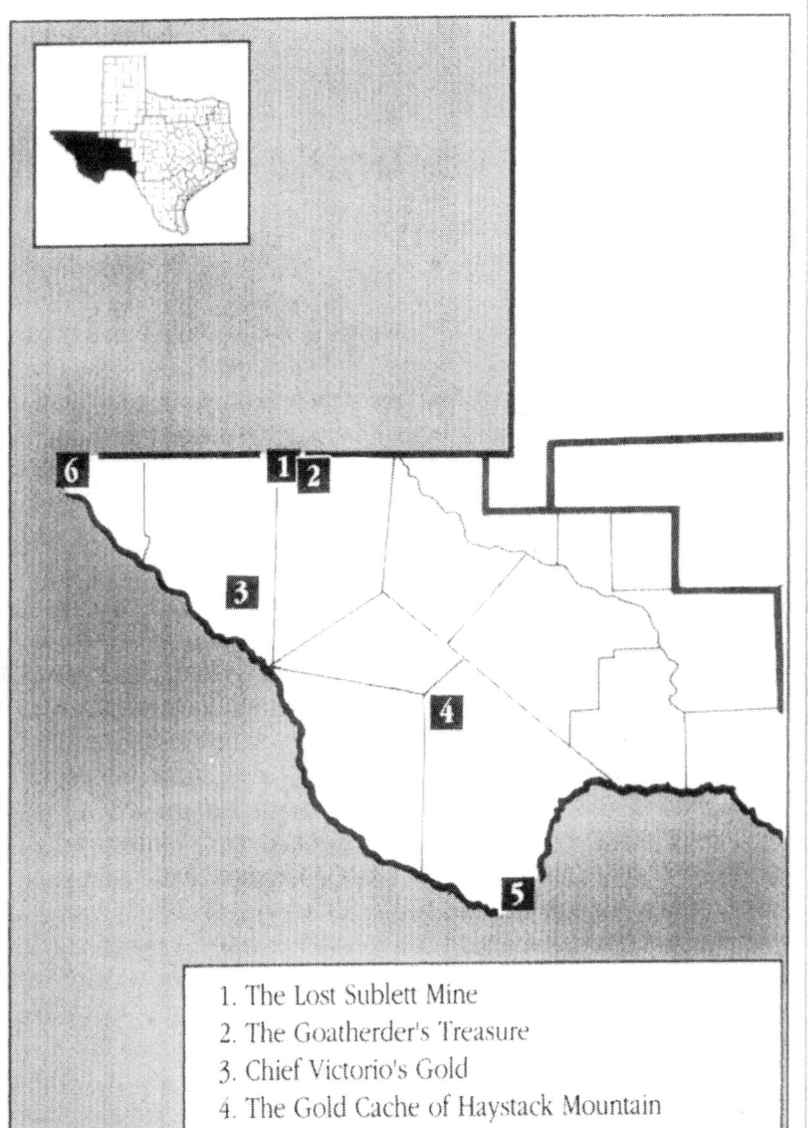

The Lost Sublett Mine

William Caldwell Sublett was a poor soul whose life was always speckled with hard luck and trouble, but he may have discovered one of the richest gold mines in all of Texas.

As a young man growing up in Tennessee, he drifted from one job to another, never able to remain very long at any of them. His wanderings took him to Missouri, where he met and married Laura Louise Denny. They traveled to Colorado, but Sublett never succeeded at anything he tried there. The two wandered from place to place looking for work, and eventually their travels took them to Bowie County, Texas, where Sublett was able to find part-time employment. Finally, discouraged at nearly every turn, he and his wife departed for West Texas, lured by the reports of opportunities in the Trans–Pecos.

The call of West Texas was strong, and after several weeks of travel they arrived in Monahans. By this time, they had run short of money and were too exhausted to continue. On the outskirts of Monahans, the Sublett family set up housekeeping out of the back of their wagon and in an old shabby tent. While Sublett looked for odd jobs around town, his wife took in washing.

When Sublett wasn't whitewashing buildings or mopping out saloons, he took prospecting trips in the rugged Guadalupe Mountains about a hundred miles to the west. He was often warned of the hostile Apaches who lived in the mountain range, but oblivious to danger, he went anyway.

Because of his disregard for the menace of the Apaches, his eccentric behavior, his inability to hold a job for long, and his ragged clothes, Sublett soon got the reputation of being a bit crazy. People regarded him as another demented old prospector who had spent too much time out in the West Texas sun and who was always looking for a handout. He was known around Monahans as "Old Ben."

Years passed, and the Subletts had three children: two girls, Ollie and Jeanne, and a boy, Rolth. As the children grew, Mrs. Sublett worried that the wild environs of the Monahans cowtown was not a proper place for them to be raised. This and Old Ben's inability to hold a job gave the family the impetus to move to Odessa, a larger town some twenty-five miles to the east. Odessa was a growing center of economic and ranching activity, and while still possessing an element of wildness, it provided a more suitable cultural climate in which to raise the children.

Soon after the move, Laura Louise Sublett died. She had suffered for a long time from tuberculosis and gradually grew weaker and weaker, succumbing just six months after Rolth's birth. Ollie, the older daughter, took over the washing business and assumed responsibility for raising her younger brother and sister. The family's living was meager as Old Ben made the rounds of Odessa, taking on the occasional odd job that fell his way. The reputation he had garnered in Monahans followed him to the larger town, and with his decrepit appearance and his ramshackle wagon pulled by two pitiful horses, he was the target of cruel jokes by the townspeople.

Old Ben continued to prospect the Guadalupe Mountains, a hundred miles northwest of Odessa, even though Apache hostility was greater than ever before. The lure of this wild mountain range was strong, and it pulled at Old Ben, drawing him to the dark canyons time and again. The massive limestone peaks and the deep shaded valleys of the Guadalupe Mountains never suggested the existence of gold or any other kind of ore in the aged and crumbling beds of sedimentary rock, but Old Ben kept searching. He always came back from the mountains with his scalp, but his repeated visits added to his reputation as a crazy man.

Old Ben told everyone in Odessa he was about to strike it rich, and when he did, he would buy drinks for the entire population of the town. He claimed that one day he would return from the Guadalupes a wealthy man. To the townspeople, he was just feeble Old Ben, tolerated like any other strange coot.

Old Ben began hanging around with an aged Apache while living in Odessa. The two met while both were employed whitewashing a building. The Apache, like Old Ben, was down on his luck and lived hand-to-mouth doing odd jobs and taking handouts. During a break at painting one day, the old Indian told Sublett he knew the location of a rich gold placer mine in the Guadalupe Mountains. Sublett pressed him for details and made a rough map based on the old man's description. Soon after, Old Ben's trips to the mountains became more and more frequent. He was certain he could find the placer mine described by the Apache, and his quest to do so became an obsession.

Sublett's endless searching meant he neglected his family. Before long, the only money they had was what Ollie brought in from washing. Several of the leading women of the town starting calling for the authorities to take the children away from the crazy old prospector and place them in homes where they could be properly cared for and taught to lead decent lives.

About a week after an attempt to remove the Sublett children to foster homes, Old Ben returned from one of his trips to the Guadalupe Mountains, pulled his creaky old wagon up to the Mollie Williams Saloon in downtown Odessa, walked in, and poured out a buckskin pouch full of gold nuggets! He loudly ordered drinks for everyone in the place. That done, he announced that he had just found the richest gold mine in all of North America. Old Ben, the crazy old bum, was now a wealthy celebrity in Odessa.

The next day, he found proper accommodations for his three children and outfitted them with new clothes for the first time in their lives. Life had taken a positive turn for Old Ben and his children.

Within three weeks, Old Ben found himself low on funds and began making plans for another trip to the mountains. He hitched up his team and struck out as before, returning in a few days with several more pouches of gold nuggets. One man who saw the gold described it as being so pure a jeweler could hammer it out easily.

Whenever the need arose, Old Ben made a trip to the mountains, and each time he returned, his standard of living would rise. Many of the citizens of Odessa tried to pry the secret of the location of the mine from Old Ben, some even offering him large amounts of money, but he remained aloof and secretive. He reminded them that not long before, they were all calling him crazy.

Sublett was often trailed. He had expected such tactics and went to elaborate lengths to throw the trackers off his trail. He would leave Odessa at odd hours of the night. Sometimes he would set up camp on the Pecos River, stay there for three or four days, and then return to Odessa. Sometimes he would elude the trackers entirely and return to town in a few days with more sacks of gold.

Sublett kept his money in a bank in Midland owned by W.E. Connell. Connell observed that whenever Sublett's account ran low, the old man would make another trip to the Guadalupe Mountains. Within a week, Sublett would arrive at Midland and invariably deposit cash. Connell never found out where Sublett exchanged his gold for money, and it remains a mystery to this day.

Connell and a Midland rancher named George Gray often talked about Old Ben and his gold mine in the Guadalupes. Together, the two offered Sublett ten thousand dollars if he would reveal the location of the mine to them, but Sublett laughed at this proposition and told them he could go out to his mine and dig up that much in less than a week.

Connell and Gray began to meet every evening to discuss ways to find out the location of the mine. They soon hit upon a scheme. They hired a local cowboy named Jim Flannigan to track Sublett to the mine and then report back to them with the location.

When Sublett's account began to run low within the next few weeks, Connell and Gray alerted Flannigan that the old man would make a trip to the mountains at any time. Lee Driver, the owner of a Midland livery stable and an accomplice of Connell and Gray, kept a horse ready for Flannigan to take at a moment's notice.

After about two weeks of waiting, Sublett was spotted leaving Odessa in a carriage pulled by two burros. Alerted in Midland, Flannigan picked up Old Ben's tracks just north of Odessa. The carriage tracks were easy to follow in the soft West–Texas sand that covers much of the Trans–Pecos, and Flannigan had no trouble staying on the trail. He remained behind and just out of sight of Sublett for nearly seventy-five miles, but somewhere on a stretch of the trail that paralleled the Pecos River, Flannigan lost him.

Frantic, he circled the area several times trying pick up some trace of the wagon and burros but had no luck. While he was trying to find the trail again, Flannigan encountered a hunter who said he had seen Sublett heading back into Odessa. Flannigan, feeling he had been tricked, turned and spurred his mount toward Odessa, but before he got there, Sublett had already returned. The morning of the next day, Old Ben deposited a large sum of money in Connell's bank.

As the story of Old Ben's trickery made the rounds, people began to assume the old man had a cache of ore or money located somewhere along the Pecos River.

A year or two passed, and Old Ben made the acquaintance of another old prospector, who went by the name of Grizzly Bill. As Old Ben did not have many friends and the two men were very much alike, an instant kinship formed.

It has been said that Old Ben eventually revealed the location of his mine to Grizzly Bill, telling him there was more gold than he could ever use in a lifetime and he wanted to share it with someone.

With Old Ben's directions, Grizzly Bill apparently found the mine. On one of his return trips from the Guadalupe Mountains, he stopped at a tavern in Pecos to show off his new-found riches, initiating a celebration that lasted well into the night. He took on more liquor than he could hold and got himself talked into a bronc-riding contest. He was thrown and died instantly from a broken neck.

Another time, on returning from a trip to the Guadalupes, Old Ben ran into an acquaintance named Mike Wilson. He showed Wilson several sacks of gold nuggets and, apparently in a generous mood, gave him directions to the mine. Wilson, like Old Ben and Grizzly Bill had done, arrived back in Odessa several days later with about a half-dozen canvas ore bags filled with gold. Unable to contain his glee, Wilson announced his discovery, bought everyone within earshot several rounds of drinks, and launched a party that lasted three days. At the end of that time, Wilson found that nearly all his gold was gone, so he decided to go back for another load. During his second trip to the placer mine, Wilson became confused and disoriented and could not remember the directions given him by Sublett. He mixed up landmarks and got lost. Eventually, he returned to Odessa and asked Old Ben to give him the directions again.

Sublett was incensed at Wilson's carelessness; he called him a fool and said he could not be trusted with the directions to the mine.

Mike Wilson spent the better part of the rest of his life searching for the rich mine he had once found. Eventually he died in a small cabin in the foothills of the Guadalupe Mountains, at the last still trying to find the lost Sublett mine.

There is another story, that sometime around 1895, Rufus Stewart was doing some remodeling on a house for Judge J.J. Walker of Barstow, California. Stewart had once been a guide for immigrants heading west to California and had also been a driver for the Overland Mail. He had led an adventurous life and been involved in several skirmishes with renegade Apaches in and around the Guadalupe Mountains. Now he relished telling the tales of his youth in the wild west, and he was never at a loss for listeners. One day, while taking a break from his remodeling job, he found a listener in Judge Walker himself, who was sipping lemonade in the shade of a big elm tree on the front lawn. Stewart joined the judge and unfolded another chapter in the story of the lost Sublett mine.

Stewart said that in 1888, several officials of the Texas and Pacific Railroad hired him to guide them on a hunt into the Trans–Pecos area. Stewart led the men to a place near the Pecos River he knew to be a favorite feeding ground for deer and pronghorn. Word reached the hunting party that several Mescalero Apaches had broken free from a reservation in New Mexico to the north and were heading for the very place Stewart and his party were encamped. Stewart, who had his young son with him, was naturally cautious and had guards posted around the camp each evening.

One night while he was on guard duty, Stewart watched as a wagon pulled by a single horse approached the camp. Confidently, the driver steered the wagon right into camp and stepped down. Stewart recognized Ben Sublett, whom he had met previously in Odessa. Stewart was aware of Old Ben's eccentric behavior and the stories of his gold mine. He invited Ben to have coffee with him and spend the night, and soon several of the Texas and Pacific Railroad men awoke and joined them. They all visited around the campfire for another hour, but as the night wore on, the railroad men went back to their tents.

When they were alone, Sublett told Stewart he was on his way to his gold mine in the Guadalupe Mountains. He also said this would probably be his last trip, as he was getting on in years and now had all the wealth he knew what to do with. He told Stewart that if he wanted to go along, he would take him to the mine.

Stewart told Sublett that he could not leave the men he had been entrusted to guide, and that he had serious misgivings about taking his young son into hostile Apache territory. Sublett said he would never be bothered by Apaches as long as he was with him. Stewart, however, decided to remain in the camp.

Morning came, and after feeding Sublett a good breakfast, Stewart rode several miles with him to the top of what he has since described as a blue mound toward the west. From this point, Sublett, with the aid of a telescope, tried to show Stewart the approximate location of the mine. Stewart said Sublett told him that if he would go with him, he would take him right to the mine, but that if he went alone, he probably would not find it. The two men shook hands, and Sublett promised he would return in three days.

True to his word, Sublett drove the wagon into the hunters' camp on the evening of the third day, and as soon as the railroad men bedded down, he poured a large quantity of gold nuggets onto a deer hide he had unrolled by the light of the campfire.

Stewart remarked that all of the nuggets were of an uncommonly large size. Sublett said that was because the larger ones were easier to pick up and he left the smaller ones lying where he found them. Just another rake through the gravel, he said, would yield several more of the large ones.

The next morning after breakfast, Sublett left for home. That was the last time Stewart saw him. Not many weeks afterward, Stewart tried to find the Sublett mine using the directions provided by Old Ben. He rode to the blue mound and tried to recall the landmarks Sublett had described. He made several forays into the Guadalupe Mountains, but he never found the gold.

Old Ben was known to share the secret of his famous gold mine with only one other person, his son Rolth, when he lowered the boy into the mine with a length of rope. As a grown man, Rolth tried for many years to find the mine but was never successful.

Throughout the remainder of his life, Old Ben Sublett lived comfortably and provided well for his children. When he died in Odessa in 1892, he did not leave much of the wealth he had brought out of the Guadalupe Mountains, but he did leave a legacy.

Some researchers dispute the notion that Old Ben Sublett ever actually had a gold mine in the Guadalupes. Those who have studied the geology of this mountain range have concluded that the weathered sedimentary structure of what was once an undersea algae reef is not conducive to the formation of gold ore. Gold, they tell us, is a result of the deposition of hydrothermal solutions under pressure that penetrate into the rock surrounding an underground pocket of molten material. In order for gold to form, there must first be some type of volcanic activity beneath the surface. According to geological records, no such activity has been detected in the Guadalupe Mountains.

It is entirely within the realm of possibility, however, that deep within the layers of limestone that make up the Guadalupes can be found evidence of ancient volcanic activity. Just a few miles to the west of the Guadalupe Mountains are several mountains of volcanic origin, and a 1987 geographic expedition into the Guadalupes noted evidence of intrusive igneous rock on the southeast-facing slope—in the approximate area where it is believed the Lost Sublett Mine is located.

Other investigators suggest that Sublett did not have a mine at all but rather stumbled onto an ancient Spanish gold cache left by the Conquistadors who explored and mined much of the southwest. Still others suggest that Old Ben discovered a Mescalero Apache gold cache. Both Geronimo and Mangas Coloradas, noted Apache chieftains, have stated that the Guadalupe Mountains were the source of the gold of the Mescaleros.

The notion has also been advanced that Sublett actually participated in holdups of mail and freight wagons traveling between El Paso and points east and that his gold represented booty he had taken in these robberies.

Whatever the source of the gold, people are still involved in the search for the Lost Sublett Mine of the Guadalupe Mountains. Today, much of the mountain range lies within the boundaries of a national park and treasure hunting is forbidden by law, but these laws are not important to those who come for the search, for the dream, for the chance to be the one to discover Old Ben's lost placer mine.

The Goatherder's Treasure

The Guadalupe Mountains of West Texas are notable for several reasons: the 8,751 foot Guadalupe Peak is the highest point in the Lone Star State; the Butterfield Overland Mail and Stagecoach Company constructed a route through Guadalupe Pass and transported mail, payrolls, and passengers during 1858–59; the range was the last stronghold of the Mescalero Apaches until they were driven from the region in 1870 by the U.S. Cavalry under Lt. Howard Cushing; and these majestic mountains are the setting for some of the most tantalizing tales of lost mines and buried treasures in Texas, perhaps in the entire United States.

Before white settlers came to the region, native grasses were rich and plentiful and, according to one account, grew as "high as the hips of a tall horse." Because of the grasses, white settlers found the area ideal for grazing livestock, and soon several small cattle- and sheep-ranching operations were established in the shadows of the Guadalupe Mountains.

Early in this century, a man named J.C. Hunter saw the front range of the Guadalupes as having great potential, and he purchased thousands of acres of land in the area. Hunter moved large herds of Angora goats onto the land. Demand was great then for mohair, the yarn made from the long, silky hair of this goat, and those who could keep the eastern markets supplied with it were making good profits. Hunter believed he could make a fortune with a successful Angora goat-ranching operation in the Guadalupe Mountains, and history has proven him correct.

J.C. Hunter's ranch became one of the finest in the region. It was stocked with cattle and sheep as well as goats. He employed several dozen cowboys and goat- and sheepherders on the front range of the Guadalupe Mountain escarpment.

One of the goatherders who worked for Hunter was young Jesse Durán. Jesse, along with his parents and siblings, had migrated from the interior of Mexico two years earlier, crossed the Rio Grande into Texas, and come north in search of work on one of the prosperous ranches springing up in the region. A skilled herder in his native Mexico, Jesse found employment on the Hunter Ranch, and was soon placed in charge of a large herd of goats which grazed the eastern limits of the ranch.

Jesse was an uncomplicated, uneducated young man who never owned much of any value during his short lifetime. With his job on the Hunter Ranch, his basic needs for food and shelter were satisfied, and he longed for little else. Though he received a small salary, Jesse had little need for money. One day in the spring of 1930, Jesse Durán accidentally discovered a cache of fabulous wealth in a shallow limestone cave in the Guadalupe Mountains, a discovery that was to change his life and set in motion searches for a rich treasure that continue today.

Jesse was with his herd one misty spring morning when he noted his canteen was empty. The goats were grazing contentedly along the top of Rader Ridge, a narrow, low limestone ridge that juts out from the southeast escarpment of the Guadalupe Mountains and extends toward the El Paso–Carlsbad highway some two miles distant. It had been raining for two days, a cold rain with a brisk wind. Jesse, wrapped in a warm, worn woolen poncho, watched his goats from the sparse shelter of a madrone tree. Presently, he decided to walk over to nearby Juniper Spring to fill his canteen.

Juniper Spring was about a mile southwest and downhill from where Jesse sat. He turned into the wind and struck out for the spring. After a few minutes on a narrow goat trail, Jesse decided to try a shortcut across a gently-sloping limestone outcrop. The route would shorten his walk, but it proved to be considerably rougher than the trail. Large slabs of weathered limestone rock lay everywhere, and Jesse walked around and on top of many of them. Once, as he stepped onto a rain-slicked slab of rock, it gave way under him and slid downslope, spilling him to the ground. When the goatherder rose and wiped the mud and desert debris from his pants and poncho, he noticed a small opening in the outcrop where the large flat rock had rested.

In the dim light of the cloudy morning, Jesse peered into the opening and realized he was looking into a shallow cave. As his eyes became accustomed to the dark interior, Jesse recoiled from what he saw. Just inside the opening, propped up in seated positions against the right wall, were three skeletons with what was left of their rotted clothes hanging loosely from the bones. Leaning against the opposite wall of the cave were several rifles. He saw something else: on the floor of the small cavern were several strong-boxes of the type used by Wells Fargo and the Butterfield Overland Mail. One of the boxes was open, and Jesse saw that it was filled with hundreds of gold and silver coins.

He touched nothing in the cave. Indeed, he refused to enter the small opening. Frightened, he replaced the limestone slab over it. He went on to Juniper Spring and filled his canteen. He returned to his herd on the ridge and pondered what to do with his discovery.

Later that afternoon, Jesse decided to tell the ranch foreman what he found. Making certain his goats were secure, he walked the several miles to the home of Frank Stogden, arriving about an hour past sundown. Mrs. Stogden greeted Jesse at the back door and invited him in out of the rain and cold for some coffee. She told the young man that Stogden and three neighboring ranchers were playing cards in another room and would see him as soon as they were finished.

In about an hour, Stogden called Jesse in, and he and the three ranchers listened to the story of his incredible discovery. Stogden and his friends were ready to ride out at first light and recover the treasure, but Jesse seemed hesitant. He told the men he feared the spirits of the dead which he believed possessed the cave and watched over all that was inside it. Jesse was a devout Catholic with a strong belief in the power of departed souls. He also believed that any treasure found with skeletons was destined to remain where it was, and any who disturbed the site would bring hardship and even death to themselves and their families. Jesse sincerely believed that nothing but evil would result from a return to the treasure cave. As he haltingly told his fears to the four men, he became very apprehensive.

The ranchers questioned Jesse about the location of the cave, but the young herder's fear made them cautious, for they did not want to risk further refusal. The men agreed to wait until the next morning to discuss the matter once again, and Stogden offered his barn for Jesse to sleep in that night. In the morning, he told the young man, they would talk some more and perhaps ride out to the treasure cave and examine it.

The next morning, Jesse Durán was gone and was never again seen in the vicinity of the Guadalupe Mountains.

Stogden and the three other men arrived by horseback at Juniper Spring around mid-morning of the next day. The rain had obliterated all sign of Jesse's presence, so the men dismounted, hitched their horses to trees, and began combing the rugged area on foot.

According to Jesse's story as it was recounted by the men many years later, the young goatherder found the small cave while hiking downslope from Rader Ridge toward the spring. Leaving the old narrow goat trail, Jesse had walked several yards along a limestone outcrop when he slipped on the large flat rock slab. Jesse had told the men that as he stood in front of the cave opening, he was about a quarter of a mile due northeast of Juniper Spring.

The four ranchers searched all day but found nothing. On several occasions, they encountered large flat limestone slabs, but when they shifted them to one side, there was no cave beneath any of them. For several months the four men visited the region to look for the cave, but they eventually abandoned the search.

Many others heard the tale of Jesse Durán's incredible discovery, and soon the hills between Rader Ridge and Juniper Spring were covered with treasure hunters. In spite of all the efforts to locate the treasure, the mysterious cave still remains hidden somewhere on the rock slope of the mountain.

Research into the story Jesse Durán told suggests that this cave may well exist and in all probability did, and still does, contain a great treasure of gold- and silver-laden strongboxes.

The Guadalupe Mountains, a massive limestone reef transecting the Texas–New Mexico border and extending for nearly two hundred miles, are pockmarked with hundreds, perhaps thousands of caves ranging in size from Carlsbad Caverns to small openings barely large enough to permit a person entrance. Within a mile of Juniper Spring, this writer has found and explored at least five such caves.

The Butterfield stage line passed less than a mile south of Juniper Spring, and the Pinery, a stage stop where the Butterfield Overland Mail horses were changed and passengers were fed, is two miles to the southwest. During its brief existence, the stage line transported money, supplies, and passengers from the east to the newly settled lands in the west. The line also carried shipments of gold and silver from western mines to brokers, banks, companies, and individuals in the east.

It is well-known that desperadoes lurked in the remote fastness of the Guadalupe Mountains, and outlaws often pounced on coaches as they labored up the steep grades toward the Pinery Station. Records show that stages were halted, passengers robbed, and strongboxes and chests containing money, gold, and silver were taken on several occasions.

Given this juxtaposition of facts, it is reasonable to conclude that the cave Jesse Durán found was a cache for goods taken from the stage line. It is more difficult to explain the presence of the three skeletons in the cave. Perhaps they were victims of the robbers, or maybe there was a falling out among the bandits and three of their members were killed and left in the cave.

Other stongboxes and chests have been found in other caves in this region, all documented and authenticated. In some instances, it has been suggested, the principals involved in one or more of the robberies were captured or killed or otherwise denied the opportunity to return to the hiding place to retrieve the loot.

Jesse Durán himself is a fundamental element pertinent to the believability of this tale. Old-timers in the region who claimed to have known Jesse each stated that he was an honest, sincere, trustworthy, and hard-working young man who was not inclined to make up stories. Jesse was well-liked and had the respect of everyone who knew him.

In researching information concerning Jesse Durán, it was discovered only recently that after his visit with rancher Stogden, the young goatherder fled on foot that same night to Carlsbad, New Mexico, some seventy-five miles to the northeast. He went to the home of his sister where he related his experience. Jesse stayed hidden at his sister's home for nearly three months, rarely leaving the house during daylight hours.

Jesse's fear of the spirits of the dead was so strong that he continued to believe his accidental discovery of the treasure might bring bad luck upon his family. So greatly did he fear it that he eventually decided to leave his sister's home and go to California. There, Jesse Durán worked as a farm laborer until the day of his death, sometime in the early 1970s.

There is some evidence that others may have also found the treasure cave. Sam Hughes operated a successful cattle and sheep ranch in Dog Canyon on a northern portion of the Guadalupe Range. One day, Hughes was deer hunting with several friends near Juniper Spring when he accidentally slipped into the opening of a small cave. Hughes knew that such caves were often resting places for rattlesnakes, so he immediately extricated himself from the hole and went on with his hunt. At the time Hughes was unaware of the story of Jesse Durán's treasure cave.

Later that evening as Hughes and others were relating the day's activities around a campfire, the rancher told the story of his fall. Noel Kincaid, then foreman of the vast Hunter Ranch empire and occasional searcher for the treasure, asked Hughes to describe the cave and its location. His description of the small hole matched that of Jesse Durán given several years earlier. Hughes also said the cave was about a quarter of a mile northeast of Juniper Spring!

The next morning, the deer hunters went back to the area, but Hughes could not find the cave.

One day in 1966, camping in the Guadalupe Mountains, I met a man named Lester White, a white-bearded, wind- and sun-wrinkled outdoorsman—a throwback to the days of grizzled prospectors who lived for months at a time in and around promising strikes. Instead of a pack mule, however, White negotiated an old rusted pick-up truck around the countryside, investigating promising sites and tracking down leads relating to old legends of lost mines. White had spent fifteen years searching for treasure in the Guadalupe Mountains. At the time I met White, the Jesse Durán story was not widely known, and White was not acquainted with it.

Sharing a cup of coffee one evening in my camp, White told of finding "a little cave in a rock outcrop about a mile northeast of the Frijole ranch house and not too far from a spring." Frijole was the shaded site of the original home of rancher J.C. Hunter, and at the time was the home of ranch foreman Noel Kincaid.

White said he found this small cave quite by accident while he was resting one evening near "an old goat trail that led from the spring on up to Rader Ridge." He said that just below where he sat, odd shadows cast by the setting sun from a large flat limestone rock suggested a hole immediately adjacent to it. Approaching the rock, White noted that it had apparently slid several inches down the slope, revealing the opening to a small cave. White, a small, thin, frail man, was unable to move the rock any further, and so had to peer into the cave through the tiny space between the slab and a corner of the opening. What Lester White saw caused the hair on the back of his neck to stiffen. Inside the little cave, he said, "was at least two skeletons and a bunch of old rotted clothes and boots." White claimed he had found skeletons in these mountains on previous occasions and so was not particularly interested in these. He turned from the small cave and resumed his hike.

Taking another sip of coffee, I related the story of the treasure cave discovered by Jesse Durán. When I finished, I asked White if he thought he could find the small cave again. He assured me he could, and that evening we made plans to hike to Juniper Spring at sunrise the next morning.

From Juniper Spring, Lester White confidently walked northeast. His determined look and purposeful stride suggested he had no doubt as to the location of the treasure cave. I matched him step for step, great anticipation lending a sense of urgency to our mission. Both of us silently imagined the moment we would enter the cave and feel the coolness of gold and silver coins between our fingers.

Arriving at a prominent limestone outcrop, White paused and scanned the area carefully. "Looks different this morning," he said, somewhat less confident than he had seemed earlier.

We walked onto the outcrop. Limestone slabs were everywhere, dozens of them. Here and there could be seen small holes eroded into the bedding planes of the rock strata from ages of ground water movement. Slowly, yet with incredible efficiency, the carbon dioxide-laden ground water dissolves the highly soluble calcium carbonate in the sedimentary rock creating spaces which, given time, evolve into caves. White and I examined several of the small openings but found nothing.

From time to time, White would look up at the sun and then scan the outcrop. "The angles and shadows are different," he said several times. "Everything looks different."

White and I lifted, pried, and slid dozens of limestone slabs from their resting positions on the ground. Under none of them did we find the opening to a cave.

All day long we worked and sweated in the West Texas sun, stopping only to take a sip of water or chew on a dry tortilla. By late afternoon, we were exhausted, but White refused to give up. Getting more and more irritated as the day wore on, White tried to locate the spot where he was resting when he first saw the cave. He could not find it.

Like Lester White, others, including me, have been fooled by the angles and shadows of the desert mountains. I once discovered a small crevice in the face of a limestone rock wall about a half mile from Juniper Spring. In it was a small cache of old tools, a pair of spurs, and some other frontier artifacts. I retrieved a hand-forged axe blade but left the rest, intending to return in the near future. When I came back, I could not find the crevice! I had explored this area at least twenty times in the past and knew it well. I knew I was within fifty feet of the entrance to the crevice, but still it eluded me.

The angles and shadows were different. The sun was in a different place in the sky and made a different set of patterns on the wall of the mountain. The desert had tricked me. Others who explore the mysteries and landscapes of the desert have commented on the constantly changing face it presents, the different personalities it seems to possess and reveal to the traveler. Still others talk about the angles of the sun and the strange dance of shadows on the earth, each moment evolving into another, all different, all elusive.

I suspect this is the case with the lost Jesse Durán treasure cave. Someday, when the angles and shadows are just right, someone will stumble onto the small cave with its grisly skeletons and strongboxes filled with a fortune in gold and silver coins.

Chief Victorio's Gold

In September of 1958, as I entered my junior year at Ysleta High School in far West Texas, my Spanish teacher was Miss Myrtle Love. This would be her last year of teaching, and she was looking forward to her retirement. I dropped by to visit with her the day before school began. I knew she was interested in stories about the people and places of West Texas, and I wanted to tell her of a summer camping expedition I took, spending several days exploring around the old settlement of Indian Hot Springs some ninety-five miles downriver from El Paso on the Rio Grande. The settlement was interesting in that it was a major route used by cattle rustlers in moving stolen livestock into Mexico and was also a favorite camp for the great Apache chief Victorio. All of the seven springs were still flowing, and most of the original buildings were still standing.

Mrs. Love asked me if I knew the story of the lost gold of Chief Victorio, supposedly still hidden in a cave in the Eagle Mountains near Indian Hot Springs. When I said I didn't, she told an amazing story.

One day in 1929, Miss Love got a telephone call from the El Paso County sheriff. He, like most people in the area, knew of her habit of collecting stories about West Texas, and he told her there was a man in the county jail who had a very interesting tale to tell. He said he would arrange a meeting if she wished.

The man's name was Race Compton, and he had been arrested when found sleeping in a boxcar at the railroad yard. As he had no money on his person and the general appearance of a hobo, he was charged with vagrancy.

When she was admitted to the small interview room, Miss Love found an elderly man, probably in his sixties, who had the weather-worn look of one who had spent his life out-of-doors. He was bewhiskered and had gone too many weeks without a haircut. His hands were calloused and hard from years of work, but they were steady. He was well-mannered and spoke in a measured tone when he told Miss Love how he came to be in El Paso.

He was there, he said, to obtain some dynamite and digging equipment which he needed to gain entry to a sealed-up cave that reputedly contained millions in gold. As he spoke, Mrs. Love recorded his story.

In 1859, stagecoach lines were doing a brisk business in West Texas carrying mail, payrolls, and sometimes gold. Throughout the Trans-Pecos region was a network of stations to provide fresh horses for the coaches and meals for the passengers and drivers. One such station had been built at Eagle Springs, Texas, in the northern foothills of the Eagle Mountains some fifteen miles southwest of Van Horn and twelve miles northeast of Indian Hot Springs.

Bigfoot Wallace, who later gained fame as a daring and adventurous Texas Ranger, was a driver on one of these coaches, and his partner was a man named Joe Peacock. Though Peacock was only nineteen years old, he had been involved in several skirmishes with outlaws and Indians and had killed several men. During this time, Apache raiders were particularly active in this part of West Texas, and Chief Victorio, the leader of the Mescalero Apaches, had a reputation for hating all white men.

Minutes after the stage pulled into the Eagle Springs station, Victorio and a band of some twenty warriors charged out of the mountains and attacked. Two passengers and one of the men who operated the station were killed, several horses were taken, and Peacock, who had been struck in the leg by an arrow, was thrown across the back of a horse and taken captive by the raiders.

Traveling day and night without stopping, the Indians rode straight to their stronghold in the Tres Castillos Mountains in northern Chihuahua, some twenty miles from the Rio Grande. Here they felt safe from pursuit by the Texas Rangers and the United States Cavalry.

Peacock's wound was treated by a young Apache called Juanita who was believed to be the daughter of Victorio. It was not serious, and as soon as he was able to walk, he was forced to work in the Indian camp gathering firewood and performing other tasks normally reserved for the women.

For several months, he remained a prisoner of the Mescalero Apaches, and during that time, Juanita became more and more attracted to him. On several occasions, Victorio threatened to kill the young white man, but each time Juanita begged for his life to be spared. Eventually young Peacock was allowed to go about his camp duties without a guard, as escape from the mountain stronghold was virtually impossible.

At night, Peacock and Juanita would meet secretly, and displaying boldness uncharacteristic of an Apache woman, she tried to persuade Peacock to marry her.

But Joe was cautious. He did not want to refuse her and incur the wrath of a rejected woman who thus far was the only reason he was still alive. He did manage to delay her, saying he was very concerned about his mother back in Texas and needed to see that she was safe and well cared for. Juanita accepted this explanation but continued to press the young Texan to marry her. One night she told him that if he would agree to wed her, she would tell him where Chief Victorio hid his stolen gold.

Peacock had watched the Indians come and go often with bars of smelted gold, obviously stolen from some pack train. He knew they carried the gold bars into Mexico and used them to trade for rifles and ammunition. He had watched the tribe's artisans hammer out golden armlets and other kinds of jewelry.

When he indicated his interest in the gold to Juanita, she told him it was kept in a cave with a small opening in the Eagle Mountains near where he was captured and that one could get to it from the old Indian trail that led from Eagle Springs through the mountains toward Indian Hot Springs. Juanita said she had been in the cave many times with her father, and she remembered seeing dozens of gold bars stacked in criss-cross fashion against the back wall. In addition, she said, there were many buckskin sacks containing gold coins and nuggets. She said it would require fifty mules to transport all the gold now hidden in the cave.

She also told Peacock that Chief Victorio and several braves had recently gone to the cave to retrieve some of the gold and had encountered some soldiers along the old Indian trail. There was a brief skirmish in which one Indian was wounded and two of the soldiers were killed. Victorio feared that the white men would eventually investigate and discover the cave and the gold. Once the Indians removed what gold they needed, Victorio ordered his men to conceal the entrance with large rocks and debris so that it looked no different than the rest of the mountainside.

Being familiar with the area she described, Peacock thought he could locate the cave with no trouble. That night, he made plans to escape.

Several more weeks passed and Peacock had no opportunity to escape. Then one day, Victorio and a large contingent of warriors left for a major raiding action deep into Chihuahua, leaving only women and children in the camp. That night, Peacock met again with Juanita and promised to return for her as soon as he could. She brought a horse for him and gave him some jerked meat and a deer gut full of water.

In the dark of night, he made his way out of the mountains and across the desert. Several days later, he arrived at Eagle Springs. After resting for a week from his arduous journey, Peacock began to search for Victorio's hidden cave. He rode up and down the trail in the area described by Juanita but had difficulty interpreting the landmarks. There were several places along the trail that matched her descriptions, and they confused Peacock.

Peacock searched for days, but he was unable to locate the cave. He knew of the Apaches' skill in camouflaging a cave or mine to match the surrounding environment, but he felt as if he were on the verge of making the discovery. Weeks passed, and still he was unsuccessful.

After a while, Peacock ran out of supplies and needed to find employment. He returned to his old job with the stage line, which he kept for several more years. When he found the time, he would search for the cave, but he was becoming more and more discouraged.

Eventually Peacock earned enough money to buy a small ranch just to the north of the Eagle Mountains. He kept his job with the stage line and worked the ranch when he had time. Because he was so busy, he had very little time to search the mountains for Victorio's hidden gold.

In 1880, Peacock was riding with a company of Texas Rangers under the command of Lieutenants Baylor and North. They had gotten word that Victorio was making raids nearby, and they had responsibility for patrolling the area and keeping a watch for Apache raiders. Eventually they heard that Victorio and his band had been attacked by a force of Mexican soldiers led by General Terrazas and a full-scale battle was taking place in the plain just south of the Tres Castillos Mountains. The Ranger company crossed the river to go to the aid of the Mexicans.

By the time they arrived, the Indians had been routed and Victorio killed. (Terrazas credited one of his marksmen with bringing down the famous Apache chieftain, but the Indians claimed Victorio died by his own hand.)

During the fight with the Mexicans, twelve of Victorio's warriors along with the tribe's women and children managed to escape. When last seen, they were riding toward the Eagle Mountains. The Rangers took up pursuit.

Three days later, they encountered the Apaches in the mountains, and several skirmishes ensued between the Indians and the Rangers. The Indians were able to withstand the fierce charges of the Rangers for a while but finally ran out of food and ammunition. They made a break during the night and fled northward for the security of the Sierra Diablo Mountains. They had just entered the mountains when they were overtaken by the Rangers, and every member of the band was killed. Peacock searched the faces of the dead women for Juanita, but she was not among them. This fight marked the end of the Apache trouble in West Texas.

Years passed, and Joe Peacock was getting on in age. He retired to his ranch, and when he found the time, he would take up the search in the nearby Eagle Mountains for the elusive cave. With the passing of the years, he had forgotten most of the landmarks described by Juanita.

It was in 1895 that Joe Peacock met Race Compton. Compton was passing through Van Horn on his way to the Eagle Mountains with the intent of doing some prospecting. The two shared a common interest in gold and struck up an instant friendship. Peacock told Compton the story of Victorio's treasure, and for the next several years, the two men worked together to try to locate the cave. They remained partners for fifteen years.

In 1910, Joe Peacock died from a lingering case of pneumonia. Compton stayed on at the Peacock Ranch and continued his search for Victorio's cave. From time to time, Compton would hitchhike around West Texas in search of work in order to earn money to purchase supplies, and then he would return to the mountains until his food ran out. It was during one of his trips to El Paso to look for work and purchase some dynamite that Compton was picked up for vagrancy by the sheriff and introduced to Myrtle Love.

He confided to Miss Love that as soon as they let him out of the county jail, he was going back to the Eagle Mountains and blast open the long-concealed cave. He said he had finally found it, and that it was approximately five miles west of Eagle Springs and on the south side of the old Indian trail. He described the location as a full day's horseback ride south from Sierra Blanca and a half-day ride west out of Indian Hot Springs. Compton told Miss Love that a recent heavy rain in the area had removed a lot of the debris the Apaches had used to conceal the entrance to the cave, and all that remained was to move the large rocks blocking the entrance.

The next morning, Compton was released from the El Paso County Jail and given a ride to the city limits. He was last seen hitchhiking toward Sierra Blanca with a canvas sack of dynamite. Miss Love never heard from Race Compton again.

Was he successful in opening Victorio's long hidden cave? Did he in fact find the gold that was reputed to be hidden there? Perhaps not. It has been suggested that Compton never made it back to the Eagle Mountains. One old-timer who lived in Sierra Blanca and was familiar with the Joe Peacock story said that Compton died of a heart attack on his trip back to the mountains from El Paso. His body was found on the side of the road early one morning, his head lying atop the sack of dynamite that was to open the cave of riches he had sought for so many years. Compton was given a pauper's burial in Sierra Blanca.

There is now a historical marker at Eagle Springs where the old stage station used to be located. Aside from an occasional deer hunter, few people ever enter the harsh realm of the Eagle Mountains. The area is far from well-traveled roads and is by and large inaccessible.

Most of those familiar with the story of Chief Victorio's lost gold maintain the evidence suggests that it is still there, still hidden in a cave in the Eagle Mountains.

The Gold Cache of Haystack Mountain

A few miles northwest of Alpine, Texas, in or near Haystack Mountain, may lie one of the richest gold caches that ever existed in West Texas.

The Lost Haystack Mine, as it is called by locals, came to notice around 1930 when a man hiked to the mountain and returned the same day with a knapsack full of gold nuggets. Though few doubt the existence of the gold, its location remains a mystery, as does the man who extracted its riches for so many years.

According to several Alpine residents, the cache was accidentally discovered around the turn of the century by a sheepherder named Mister Johns. Mister Johns, a half-breed Seminole–Negro, was well known for his skill and dependability as a sheepherder and had worked for several ranchers in the area over the previous thirty years.

Mister Johns had originally come to Texas from his home in Coahuila, Mexico. Johns was descended from the original band of Seminole–Negroes who settled in Coahuila in the early 1830s. They had escaped the hardships of the forced march from their homelands in south Florida, a time in history known as the Trail of Tears, and fled to the seclusion of northern Mexico, far from the pursuit of the American soldiers. The Seminole–Negroes, along with members of the Chickasaw and Cherokee tribes, established settlements in the harsh desert environment, initiated farming and ranching enterprises, and soon prospered. During succeeding years, as West Texas was being settled, many of the descendants of these Indians, like Mister Johns, migrated northward seeking work on the ranches that were being established in this remote and rugged part of the Southwest.

In the early years of the century, Mister Johns lived with his wife of several decades in a modest shack between Alpine and Haystack Mountain. All his children were grown and living in the area, working for other ranchers. Mister Johns had several grandchildren, but his favorite was Jim Johns. Since he was old enough to walk, young Jim Johns had followed his grandfather around, helping him tend to the sheep. Often the two would ride out to Haystack Mountain for a picnic or to do some hunting.

Mister Johns was described by those who claimed to have known him as quite tall and almost comically thin. Well over six feet tall, the half-breed sheepherder was reputed to have weighed less than one hundred pounds.

One rainy day, Mister Johns was looking for some strayed sheep in the area of Haystack Mountain. He was on horseback in a narrow canyon when the storm took a turn for the worse. Mister Johns got off his horse, tied it to a tree, and sought shelter in a narrow opening in the canyon wall. As he squeezed his thin frame into the crack, he saw it was the entrance to a small cavern that extended deeper into the mountain. Mister Johns explored the passageway.

The thin shaft ran about ten yards before opening up into a small room about six feet square with a ceiling just high enough to permit Johns to stand upright. Stacked along one wall of the small room were numerous leather sacks. Mister Johns knelt to examine the sacks and saw they were covered with a deep layer of dust, evidence that they had been placed in the small cavern a long time ago. With his pocketknife, Mister Johns cut open one of the sacks.

Several handfuls of gold nuggets spilled out onto the cavern floor.

Mister Johns was excited by his find but unsure what to do about it. Being only a poor sheepherder, he was certain that if he showed up in Alpine with gold, he would be accused of having stolen it. Deciding he had little use for this metal so highly coveted by white men, Johns decided to leave it where he found it. When the storm abated, Mister Johns retrieved his horse and went home.

As Mister Johns was quite elderly, it came as no surprise when he became infirm after a few years and was confined to his bed and near death. A few days before he died, Mister Johns called Jim Johns, now a young man, to his bedside. There, with difficulty, the old man told him the story of finding the gold cache in the small cave near Haystack Mountain. Though his memory of that event several years earlier was dimmed by age and sickness, Mister Johns was able to provide some vague directions.

It took Jim Johns five years to find the gold cache. When he finally did, he filled a knapsack with nuggets, walked to the train station in Alpine, and bought a ticket to San Antonio, where he converted the gold into cash.

Jim Johns never returned to Alpine to live, apparently preferring the Alamo City. When his funds ran low, he would travel by train to Alpine, walk the several miles to Haystack Mountain, refill his knapsack, and return to San Antonio.

Jim Johns did this several times during the 1930s and was often seen going to or coming from Haystack Mountain. Johns often stopped and visited with friends in Alpine, and on several occasions, he pulled a handful of gold nuggets from his pack and showed them around, leaving no doubt as to the truth of the story of the lost cache.

In 1937, a group of men approached Jim Johns in San Antonio and attempted to strike a deal to pay him a sum of money in exchange for information on the location of the gold cache. Johns politely refused, and the men left, visibly annoyed. Several days later, the men returned with the same offer, and again Johns refused. This time the men became belligerent, an argument ensued, and Johns was shot in the stomach.

Johns survived the attempt on his life, but he never returned to the gold cache at Haystack Mountain for fear that he would be followed. About a year after recovering from his gunshot wound, Jim Johns died from a heart ailment.

To this day, it remains unclear who initially cached the sacks of gold in the small cave near Haystack Mountain. Some have suggested the wealth was hidden by the Spaniard Coronado during his explorations in the area in the sixteenth century. Others suspect it is outlaw loot taken during a robbery of an El Paso–San Antonio stagecoach run.

Several Alpine residents and local ranchers have tried, unsuccessfully, to find the elusive opening in the wall of a canyon near Haystack Mountain, an opening that leads to a fortune in gold nuggets.

The Curse of the Bill Kelley Mine

The Big Bend country of West Texas is one of the harshest landscapes in all of America. This great expanse of land is part of the Chihuahuan Desert and exhibits extreme aridity, rugged mountains, deep and mysterious canyons, and a variety of wild life, much of it poisonous or clawed. The area has been the home or hiding place of Apaches, Comanches, bandits, and Mexican raiders. Early ranchers in the Big Bend were impressed by its beauty and frustrated by its severity. This challenging environment stretches many miles into Mexico.

In 1884, the four Reagan brothers (John, Jim, Frank, and Lee) established a cattle ranch near the mouth of what is now known as Reagan Canyon in southern Brewster County. They settled in sight of the Rio Grande, which at this point is a relatively slow-flowing stream after its rapid and tortuous journey through several twisting canyons. The Reagans herded cattle up from Mexico and grazed them on the lush grasses in the area of their quiet settlement.

On occasion, the Reagans would drive cattle to the railroad loading pens at Dryden. This seventy-five mile journey to the northeast was followed by loading the animals onto cattle cars provided by the Southern Pacific Railroad. During one of these loading operations, the

Reagans met Bill Kelley, a Seminole–Negro who had walked from the old Seminole settlement in northern Coahuila, Mexico. He was only nineteen, unable to read or write, dressed in rags, and looking for work. He told the Reagans he was a good man with horses, and as they needed help on the ranch, they hired him on the spot.

Kelley proved to be as good a wrangler as he claimed, and the Reagans soon allowed him to go out and work the riding stock on his own. One evening Kelley arrived late for supper after rounding up several horses that had strayed to the Mexican side of the river. He told those already gathered at the table he had found a gold mine during the search for the animals. The men, assuming that Kelley wouldn't know the slightest thing about gold, laughed at him.

The next day, Kelley and Lee Reagan rode out to the same area where the wrangler claimed he had found the gold mine. Once more they were searching for stray horses, and near the end of the day found themselves on a low ridge south of the Rio Grande. Kelley told Lee the mine was no more than a half mile away, and he would show it to him if he wished. Reagan said it was getting late and he was tired and thought they ought to get back to the ranch. Kelley pulled a fist-sized chunk of gold-bearing quartz from his saddlebag and showed it to Lee, saying he had dug it out of the mine. Lee, not believing it was gold, threw the rock to the ground and told Kelley he was being paid to look for horses, not gold mines.

A few weeks later, the brothers drove another bunch of cattle to the loading pens at Dryden. Here Kelley hopped a freight bound for San Antonio, telling the brothers he would return in two weeks. He entered into a conversation with the conductor, a man named Locke Campbell, and told Campbell about the mine, giving him general information about its location. When he arrived in San Antonio, he gave Campbell a small piece of the quartz as proof. Campbell said he would have it evaluated and try to get in touch with him at a later date. Kelley left another piece of the gold with an assayer in San Antonio named Fisher.

As promised, Kelley returned to the Reagan ranch within two weeks and went back to working the livestock. A few weeks passed, and Kelley received a letter from Fisher. Because Kelley was expected to be out on the range for a few more days, the brothers opened the letter and read that the gold was proclaimed to be very rich, worth perhaps $80,000 per ton. Two days later, when Kelley rode into the ranch, the cook told him that the brothers had opened and read his letter. Kelley suspected the men wanted him to lead them to the mine and then kill him. Before anyone but the cook knew he had returned, Kelley stole a horse from the corral and rode away.

After the Reagans had determined what had happened they took up Kelley's trail and tracked him for two days, but gave up the search at a point where the tracks crossed the Rio Grande into Coahuila.

After entering Coahuila, Kelley rode to the Piedra Blanca Ranch owned by George Chessman. He asked for and was offered a job and was assigned to the foreman, John Stillwell. After getting to know and trust Stillwell, Kelley related the story of the lost mine and his escape from the Reagan brothers. He told Stillwell he was afraid for his life and was thinking about returning to his relatives at the Seminole settlement. Kelley also showed Stillwell a saddlebag full of gold nuggets he claimed had come from the mine. A short time later, Kelley and a dozen other cowhands were sent to drive a large herd of cattle to Mexico City. On arriving at the capital, Kelley disappeared.

The only solid lead on Bill Kelley surfaced several decades later in the summer of 1946. Monroe Payne, a Seminole–Negro like Kelley, and eighty-four years old at the time, claimed to be a relative of Kelley and told researcher Virginia Madison that Kelley returned to the Seminole settlement in Coahuila following his trip to Mexico City. From there, he went to Oklahoma where he got involved in a bootlegging operation and subsequently went to prison. Upon being released from jail, he moved to San Antonio, where he resided until he died.

Eventually, Locke Campbell, the train conductor Kelley had told about the mine, began a search for it. When he learned of Kelley's disappearance from the Reagan ranch, he searched for him also. Once, at a cattlemen's convention in San Antonio, Campbell met Jim Reagan, and they shared experiences about Bill Kelley's lost mine. Reagan told Campbell he believed his brother could lead them to the exact spot where Kelley had told Lee about the mine.

Five years had elapsed since Kelley's disappearance when the Reagan brothers and Campbell undertook a systematic search for the lost mine. They returned to the site where Lee and Kelley had hunted horses, and from there they spread out and searched for several miles in each direction but were unable to find anything. The men decided they could do no more until they found Kelley.

They eventually located his mother at the Seminole settlement. She related how her son had returned one day with a saddlebag full of gold, remained for several weeks, and then left. The old woman did not know where he went.

The Reagan brothers resumed the search and over the next few years spent thousands of dollars and invested hundreds of hours hunting the gold mine they had laughed about when Bill Kelley first announced it.

Campbell continued to believe the key to rediscovering the lost mine was to locate Bill Kelley, and to this end, he placed advertisements in newspapers around the country and made numerous inquiries during his travels.

Around this time, a black man appeared at a store in Eagle Pass, Texas, and dumped a small bag of gold nuggets on the counter. He told the proprietor of the store that he would show him the location of a rich gold mine across the river in the Ladrones Mountains if the man would pay him one thousand dollars. The storekeeper refused but learned several months later that the man was Bill Kelley.

In response to Campbell's newspaper advertisements, reports came in from several people who either claimed to be Kelley or knew of his whereabouts. Several rumors also surfaced that Kelley had died.

On July 19, 1899, Campbell, Jim Reagan, Big Bend ranchers D. C. Bourland and O. L. Mueller, and a prospector named John Finky entered into an agreement to search for the mine. Finky was to conduct the actual search while the others provided financing. If any gold was found, it was to be shared equally by the five men.

For weeks, Finky hunted in the Ladrones Mountains on the Mexican side of the river. One day he arrived at Bourland's ranch and announced he had located the mine. He told Bourland he had come across the long-dead body of a Negro in a remote canyon in the range. Three hundred yards up the canyon and just out onto a low ridge, Finky discovered the gold mine. He showed Bourland several large pieces of nearly pure gold he had dug out of the mine. Finky wanted Bourland to assemble the others and go directly to the mine, but Bourland said it would have to wait. West Texas was in the middle of a severe drought, and the ranchers were working day and night to save their livestock. Bourland promised Finky that when the situation was under control, they would all ride to the mine.

That night as Finky settled onto the cot Bourland had provided he was stung on the face and neck by a scorpion. The next day his face had swollen so badly he had to be taken to a doctor in Sanderson. While Finky was recovering in the hospital, he was visited by Bourland and Reagan who tried to get him to reveal the location of the mine. Not trusting the two men, Finky refused. Instead, he told them it was against Mexican law for Americans to operate a mine in that country without special permission from the Mexican government. He told the men that when he recovered, he would travel to Mexico City to obtain the necessary permission and then return to lead them to the mine. Two weeks later, Finky recovered and undertook his journey to Mexico City. He traveled by train to El Paso where he was to make a connection to the Mexican capitol. He had a two-day layover in El Paso and spent most of it drinking at a local bar. He made friends with the bartender, told him about his discovery of the lost Bill Kelley mine, and asked him to accompany him to Mexico City. The bartender agreed and gave Finky a free room and all the liquor he could drink while they waited for the train. Two days later Finky was found dead.

Several years passed, and Bourland and Mueller lost interest in the mine. Jim Reagan died, and his brothers moved to Arizona to ranch. Campbell was getting old, but he continued to search for Bill Kelley and for information on the mine until his death in 1926.

One day in 1909, a man named Wattenburg arrived in the Big Bend area with a map reputedly showing the location of a gold mine in the Ladrones Mountains and spent several weeks asking area residents about the location of certain landmarks. Wattenburg claimed that a nephew, condemned to death in an Oklahoma prison, had provided the directions from which the map was made.

The nephew had gone to Mexico with four other men to steal horses. Passing through the Ladrones Mountains, the bandits ran into an old man carrying two large leather sacks of gold-laden quartz. They took the gold and told the old man they would kill him if he didn't reveal the source of the gold. The old man took them directly to a mine on top of a nearby ridge. There they found a large pile of rock debris next to a narrow shaft that led straight down. Not far into the shaft, the bandits could see the gleam of a thick vein of gold ore. Because a Mexican posse was not far behind them, the bandits made mental notes of the surrounding landmarks and then fled across the border. Before they left, they shot the old man and threw his body into a canyon.

Wattenburg soon met a man named John Young, who knew the Ladrones Mountains and Reagan Canyon. Wattenburg showed the map to Young who told him all the features were correctly placed. Young, Wattenburg, and another man named Felix Lowe entered into a partnership to search for the mine. Young went to Mexico City and obtained the necessary permission from the government to operate a mine in the Ladrones Mountains.

In 1910, the three men crossed the river. Optimism ran high, but once into the range, they realized the immensity of their undertaking. While the landmarks appeared to be accurate, the scale of measurement was not clear. The three men searched the range for three months without success.

Still hopeful of locating the mine, the men were preparing supplies for another expedition into the Ladrones Mountains when the Mexican Revolution broke out. Now the border area was swarming with Villistas, Carranzistas, and bandits, and it would have been foolhardy to attempt a journey into the mountains. The men waited several months, but no end to the revolution was in sight. Thoroughly discouraged, they abandoned the search.

Several months later, Young was interviewed by a San Antonio newspaper, and he told the entire story of the lost Bill Kelley mine. Jack Haggard, a rancher in Coahuila, read the story and wrote a letter to Young. He said Bill Kelley had worked on his ranch for several years and had told him about the gold mine. Haggard said one of his foremen, using directions Kelley had given, went to the Ladrones and apparently found the mine. He brought back several ore samples that were assayed and identified as "rich as the gold in a twenty dollar gold piece." Haggard's foreman also worked as a contractor at a nearby mine, and as he was rushing to finish his job in order to spend time digging gold in the Ladrones Mountains, he was killed in a gas explosion. Haggard told Young that he had searched for the mine himself. He believed he had it located when he was chased out of the mountains by a band of Villistas. Years later, Haggard was preparing for another expedition to the range when he was drowned in a fishing accident.

In 1915, Will Stillwell, the foreman of the Piedra Blanca Ranch, told his brother Roy, who lived in Marathon, Texas, that he had found Bill Kelley's lost mine. Returning from a cattle buying trip to Mexico, he said, they happened upon an old Indian woman who had been left out in the desert to die. Will and his partner gave her food and water and took her to the nearest settlement, where she recovered. In gratitude, she told them of a very rich gold mine and gave them directions from which they sketched a map. She told them to go to a certain canyon where they would find the stumps of several petrified trees. They were to go past the stumps and up the canyon until they reached a very large boulder. On the left side of the boulder, they would find a buried hatchet, and on the opposite side, they could dig up two saddlebags filled with gold. The mine from which the gold was taken was just a few hundred yards up the canyon and was filled with rocks and dirt.

Stillwell and his partner found the canyon with the petrified trees. On one side of the boulder, they dug up an Indian tomahawk, but they didn't find the saddlebags filled with gold. Continuing up the canyon, they emerged onto a low ridge and found the mine almost at once. It appeared to be dug straight down into the ground and was partially filled with rock and debris. The outlaws were out of water and decided to return to a spring at the bottom of the canyon before digging into the mine.

At the spring, they spied a gang of Mexican bandits entering the canyon from the lower end. The Mexicans spotted Stillwell and his companion and chased them. The two men fled into the maze of canyons and ridges that are the Ladrones Mountains. After two days of running from the Mexicans, they recrossed the Rio Grande and decided to wait for the Revolution to die down before going back to the mine.

A few weeks later, Stillwell joined the Texas Rangers and was assigned to a post in the Big Bend area. His company was given the task of protecting area ranchers from bandits crossing over from Mexico. While stopped at the small settlement of Castolón, Stillwell was shot in the back by a Mexican outlaw and died instantly.

Roy Stillwell, Will's younger brother, came into possession of the directions to the Bill Kelley mine. Several men approached Roy to get him to lead an expedition into the Ladrones Mountains to dig for the gold, but he steadfastly refused. Roy told everyone he believed there was a curse on the mine and that all who located it were destined to die. He pointed out all of the violent deaths associated with those who claimed to have found the gold. Roy had had several skirmishes with bandits in Mexico and had been shot several times. He had no wish to tempt fate further.

A group of men came to him with an offer to purchase the directions to the lost mine. Roy said he would like to think about it, but two days later, he was killed when a truck overturned on him. The directions to the lost mine were never found.

In the late 1940s, two men who identified themselves as mining engineers arrived in the area of the old Reagan ranch. For a month, they explored the Ladrones Mountains on the Mexican side of the river. They left, only to return to Big Bend several months later. They hired Ed Shirley of Marathon as a guide but never told him what they were looking for. Because they carried mining tools, Shirley assumed they were either prospecting or searching for the lost Bill Kelley mine. One day, the two men seemed excited about something they had discovered and told Shirley he would have to leave. They paid him off and sent him away.

Ed Shirley remains convinced that the two engineers discovered the Bill Kelley mine. He also wonders if they lived to spend their wealth, or if they, like so many others, fell victim to the curse.

The Lost Padre Mine

The year 1659 saw the establishment of the mission *Nuestra Señora de Guadalupe* in El Paso del Norte, now Ciudad Juárez, Mexico. As the padres supervised the construction of the church, a group of seven mission priests crossed the Rio Grande each morning and proceeded to the nearby Franklin Mountains where they labored in a rich gold mine. The ore from this mine was transported down the mountain to the river bank, where it was smelted into ingots and shipped to church headquarters in Spain.

The Franklin Mountains are a north-south range with southern foothills accommodating the spreading population of the border city of El Paso, Texas. While not as impressive as many other segments of the Rocky Mountain chain, the Franklins offer a welcome relief from the flat topography of this part of the Chihuahuan Desert.

Somewhere in the Franklin Mountains may lie one of the oldest and richest gold mines in the history of the west.

Several months after the mission was chartered, the structure was finished, complete with a thirty-five foot bell tower. Each morning, one of the friars would climb the tower and toll the bell, calling the priests to prayer. As he rang the huge bell, the friar could look across the river toward the Franklin Mountains and see the dark opening of the mine in which his brothers worked.

For several years, mission operations proceeded smoothly. Many of the local Indians were converted to Catholicism, and the mine in the Franklin Mountains produced several mule-loads of gold ore each month for the mother church in Spain. Things could not have been better for the padres.

Then one day in 1680, word came that the Pueblo Indians in New Mexico had risen up against their Spanish masters, killing many and driving the remainder out of the province. Several priests who had escaped fled south toward Mexico and along the way alerted their fellows that Pueblo Chief Cheetwah was gathering an army of Indians and was intent on eliminating Spanish rule in the region.

Fearing an attack by the Pueblos, the priests at the Juárez mission loaded all the golden vessels, chalices, candlesticks, and platters and carried them, along with a large store of gold ingots they had accumulated, across the river and up to the site of the mine for safekeeping. Legend tells that it took 250 mule-loads to transport all the mission wealth. Once the valuables were placed in the mine, the priests had dark red river silt brought up from the banks of the Rio Grande to fill the entire shaft. They took great pains to disguise the entrance so that it looked like any other part of the mountainside. They returned to the mission to defend it against the Pueblos.

It was not until 1692 that the Spanish finally subdued the Pueblo Indians and recaptured New Mexico. The Rio Grande valley near El Paso del Norte was peaceful again, but when the padres returned to the Franklin Mountains to rework the mine, they could not find it! Several priests who had worked in the mine had been transferred to other provinces, and the rest were dead. The mission priests searched for the shaft, but the entrance had been hidden too well. In time, the gold mine in the Franklin Mountains faded from the memories of the friars.

In 1881, a group of men from El Paso reportedly discovered some documents in the archives of the old mission in Juárez that indicated the existence of a rich gold mine in the Franklin Mountains. The men also claimed they had documents from church records in Spain substantiating the mine. The group financed several highly organized and well-manned expeditions into the mountains in search of the mine, but consistently met with failure.

In 1888, a man named Robinson claimed to have located the mine shaft by standing in the bell tower of the mission and looking for evidence of old trails leading up into the canyons of the Franklin Mountains. He selected a point in a canyon that could be seen from the tower, and when he went there, he discovered that a large amount of rock debris had been moved to cover a part of the rock face of the canyon. Robinson removed tons of rock and found the entrance to an ancient mine.

Receiving some small financial backing and using it to hire laborers, he removed what was described as reddish river silt clogging the shaft. Robinson and his workers labored for some time excavating the soil from the shaft before the financial support was pulled back.

In a fit of anger, Robinson had his men refill the shaft with the dirt and cover the opening once again with rocks.

In 1901, a man named L.C. Criss announced he had located the Lost Padre Mine in the Franklin Mountains. Criss had been searching fourteen years for it with the aid of an old manuscript he had found in Juárez. Criss said one could climb the ridge nearest to the mine and look down on the city of El Paso.

Criss had indeed found a shaft. The entrance had been concealed by rocks, and once the rocks had been removed, Criss saw that red river silt plugged the shaft. Criss and a work crew spent much time and effort cleaning the silt out of the shaft, and eventually opened 125 feet of the tunnel. He found several Spanish artifacts, including a spur and an ancient anvil. For a while, these artifacts were on display at the W. G. Walz Company in El Paso.

At the end of the shaft, Criss found two more tunnels, each going in opposite directions and each walled up by adobe bricks. He tore into one of them and removed fill dirt for about twenty feet. Criss saw that the old shaft was not well-supported and appeared to be dangerous. He told his foreman he was going to El Paso to buy timbers to shore up the tunnel and left instructions to keep everyone out of the shaft until he returned.

One of the workers, apparently sensing he was very close to the hidden treasure of the padres, resumed digging as soon as Criss was out of sight. In just a few moments, the shaft caved in, burying the man alive and filling most of the tunnel with collapsed rock. Out of funds and unable to proceed, Criss abandoned the digging and left El Paso, never to be heard from again.

In 1968, a Spiritualist minister named Martin, accompanied by his wife and an assistant named McKinney, arrived in El Paso from California and announced he knew where the Lost Padre Mine was and would begin digging within a few days. Reverend Martin claimed he had some ancient Spanish documents that contained the location of the mine as well as an inventory of the valuables concealed there by the padres three centuries earlier.

Martin contracted for some heavy machinery and excavation equipment, and amidst a large crowd of onlookers and two local television crews, he excavated a long trench down into the rock at a point on the mountain not far from a well-traveled road. Tons of rock were removed until the trench was finally about fifteen feet deep. At this point, Reverend Martin climbed down into the trench and dug with his hands into an accumulation of loose soil. After a few moments, the outline of a shaft could be seen. McKinney joined the Reverend, the two applied shovels to the task, and within two hours they had excavated about ten yards of fill, revealing what appeared to be a shaft that led into the mountain.

Several onlookers jumped into the trench to help with the digging, which went on for another three hours. At one point during the afternoon, however, an official arrived at the scene and pronounced the excavation hazardous as well as illegal. Following considerable arguing and pleading by Reverend Martin, the excavation was ordered halted and the trench covered. Dejected, Martin and his followers returned to California.

More than three centuries have passed since the Spanish padres mined gold in the Franklin Mountains. Hundreds have searched for the mine since then but apparently without success.

That there is gold in the mountain cannot be doubted. Residents who live in the foothills of the Franklins have been known to pan for and retrieve fine nuggets of gold washed into their back yards by the infrequent rains.

There is also some evidence that silver may have been discovered in the Franklin Mountains. The June 22, 1873, edition of the *Galveston Daily News* reported the discovery of two old shafts on the mountain and that tons of fill dirt had been excavated by a mining company. Following the removal of the dirt, according to the article, a three-foot-thick vein of silver was found. One of the shafts was reported to be one hundred feet deep and the other ninety feet. The newspaper articles also noted that the shafts were within two-and-a-half miles of the old mission in Juárez.

Some investigators of the Lost Padre Mine legend claim that when the priests buried the wealth of the church in the shaft, they also buried alive three of the padres and placed a curse on the area, dooming all nonbelievers who dare enter the mine. Several ancient shafts have been found in the Franklin Mountains, but so far, the store of golden artifacts and ingots have not been retrieved. The legend continues to live and to lure searchers for the Lost Padre Mine, and the treasure is still as elusive as it ever was.

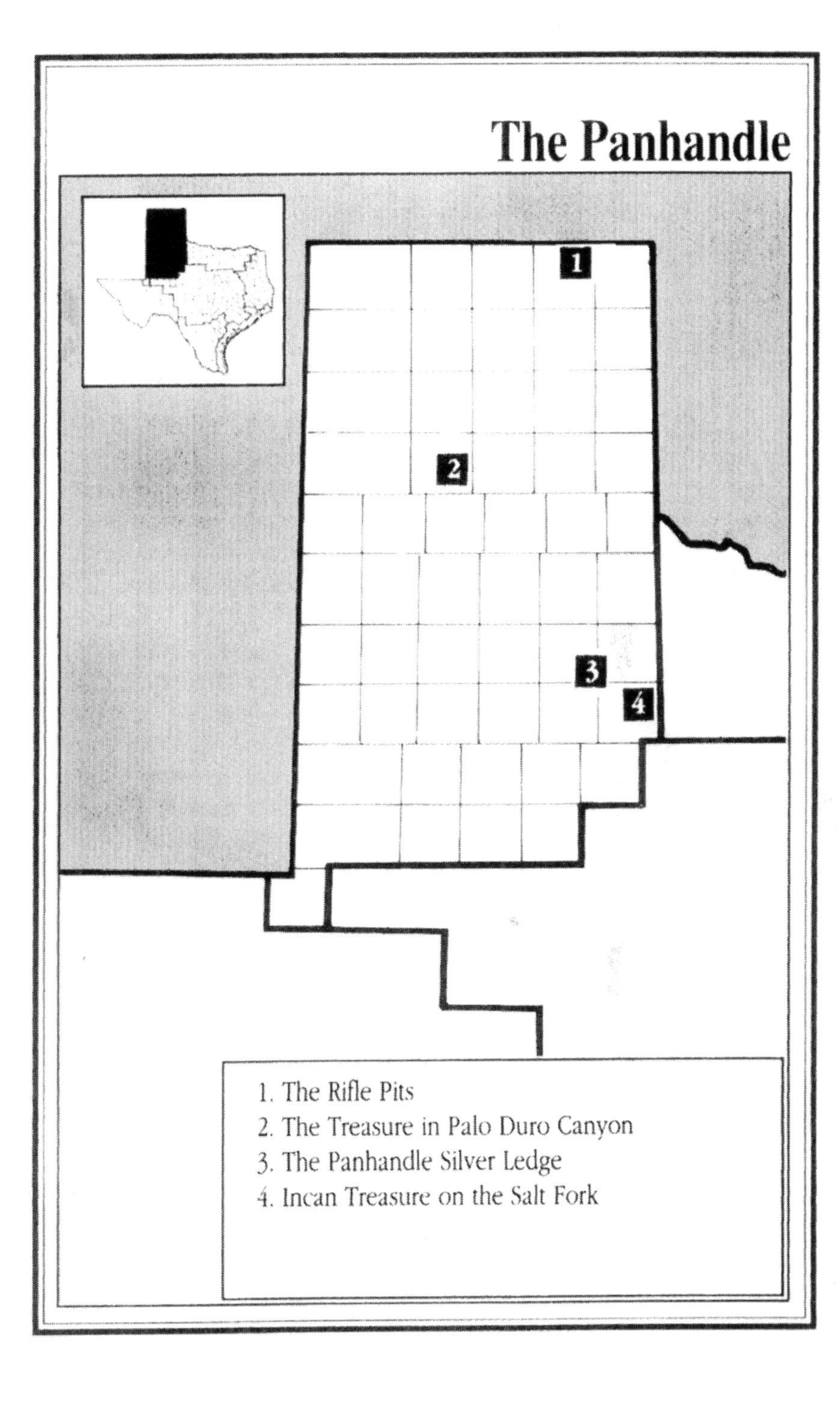
The Panhandle
1
2
3
4
1. The Rifle Pits
2. The Treasure in Palo Duro Canyon
3. The Panhandle Silver Ledge
4. Incan Treasure on the Salt Fork

The Rifle Pits

Somewhere in northeastern Ochiltree County in the Texas Panhandle lies a treasure in cached U.S. Army rifles, sabers, saddles, bottles, and other military goods. It is believed to be somewhere along the banks of Palo Duro Creek and has lain concealed for more than 120 years.

The story of the buried military cache goes back to the Medicine Lodge Treaty of 1867. Because of the failure of that treaty and the subsequent military action against the Indians, the Army assigned hundreds of soldiers to the field.

On December 1, 1868, General Eugene A. Carr took command of the Fifth Cavalry Regiment at Fort Lyon, Colorado. This group was soon joined by men from the Tenth Cavalry and eventually totaled seven hundred soldiers and service and supply personnel. Carr led the force southward to search for Indians.

The soldiers had not been on the march long before a severe blizzard struck. The storm slowed the movement of the large group of soldiers, and long before they reached a specified rendezvous point, they had run out of provisions. The weather made it difficult to hunt, and the situation was becoming serious.

One of Carr's scouts was William F. Cody, who was later to gain fame as "Buffalo Bill." Realizing the gravity of his predicament, Carr dispatched Cody to find a suitable place to set up camp and establish a supply depot. After a full day, Cody returned and led the force to a site next to

Palo Duro Creek. Here Carr was pleased to find good water and trees which could be used for fuel and construction. He expected to be resupplied by other regiments that would be moving through the area, but the severity of the storm caused him concern. Because the camp was to serve as a supply depot, Carr ordered the construction of several dugouts to house the arms and supplies.

While the soldiers set up camp, Cody and other scouts went out in search of game. Cody was not only successful in securing antelope and buffalo, he came upon a Mexican pack train eastward-bound with a load of goods for trade. Among the goods was a quantity of beer, and Cody diverted the train toward the Carr encampment on the Palo Duro Creek.

Every few days, Carr got reports from other commands, and most of them brought orders for him to remain where he was until further notice.

From this camp on the Palo Duro, Carr sent out platoons of soldiers in search of Indian renegades. Carr and his men were eager to engage the Indians, but it was not to be. Days turned into weeks, and the weather got worse. There was seldom a time when there were not six to eight inches of snow on the ground. Game grew scarcer, and the scouts were finding it difficult to provide the men with fresh meat.

As food ran out and the weather failed to improve, many of the civilian service and supply personnel abandoned the encampment. Horses and mules were dying from the cold and starvation. As if this were not enough, illness broke out among the hungry soldiers, and the regimental physician told Carr something must be done soon or it would be necessary to abandon the camp.

When things were very bleak, Cody found a large herd of buffalo. He and his men killed over a hundred of the shaggy beasts, returned with plenty of fresh meat, and saved Carr's command. Cody was regarded as a hero, and it was then that his fame and reputation began to grow.

The worst of the hardship had passed, and Carr got orders to return to Fort Lyon. Because he had lost so many mules and horses to the blizzard, he did not have enough stock to pull wagons carrying all the war materiel.

Carr decided to bury what could not be immediately taken back. The dugouts, containing hundreds of rifles, sabers, hand-blown whiskey bottles, wagons, bridles, and other military hardware, were covered and abandoned.

Carr returned safely to Fort Lyon but was never assigned to return for the buried equipment, nor was any other cavalry detachment. The U.S. Army decided the war materiel buried along the banks of Palo Duro Creek was not worth the trouble to find and recover.

Buffalo hunters who frequented this area throughout much of the 1870s had camps in the area near Palo Duro Creek. They learned of Carr's encampment and the military cache and dubbed the covered-over dugouts the "rifle pits." As the cavalry armament and hardware was useless to them in hunting buffalo, they ignored the cache, but the term "rifle pits" entered the language and is still used to identify the area.

Early settlers in the region were aware of the rifle pits but were too busy ranching to worry about what was contained in the old abandoned dugouts. Years passed, and the region grassed over and became indistinguishable from the rest of the prairie around Palo Duro Creek.

A treasure hunter came to this area some time in the 1970s looking for the rifle pits. He didn't find the rich cache, but he did find a rock on which was carved the name "W.F. Cody." The treasure hunter thought the buried fortune in historical military hardware must lie somewhere nearby . Several days of searching the area yielded nothing.

Ranchers in the region of Palo Duro Creek maintain that no one has yet found the rifle pits, and so to this day, a fortune in historical military rifles and other equipment remains concealed beneath just a few feet of Panhandle soil in Ochiltree County.

The Treasure in Palo Duro Canyon

John Casner was a moderately successful farmer in central Alabama, growing feed-corn and vegetables on modest hillside acreage. Casner's wife had died several years earlier, leaving him to raise three sons. Casner and his boys fared well in their agrarian life.

One day, news reached Casner about the gold strike in far away California. The idea of striking it rich in the gold fields had a strong appeal to the farmer, and he sold the farm and migrated west with his sons. They joined the westward trek of thousands of souls who believed they would find wealth in the far mountains.

On their way to California, the Casners passed through the Panhandle of Texas and saw the majestic landscape in and around Palo Duro Canyon. John Casner had a good feeling about this place and told his sons he would like to return here someday and establish a sheep ranch.

The family finally got to California and spent the next two years panning gold from dozens of streams in the Sierra Nevadas. They worked very hard and amassed an impressive amount of gold. They took their gold to the United States Mint at Carson City, Nevada, and exchanged it for a thousand twenty-dollar gold pieces.

With their new wealth, the Casners decided they didn't care to return to the hard work of panning gold out of cold mountain streams. John Casner recalled the rich pastures of the Texas Panhandle and suggested they return there and invest in a sheep-ranching enterprise.

In no particular hurry, the Casners hung around Carson City for a while enjoying their money. When the time had arrived to leave for the high plains of Texas, John Casner and one of his sons, Lew, caught the gold fever once again and decided to travel through Southern California, Arizona, and New Mexico prospecting. By this time, the other two sons were committed to starting a sheep ranch, so they headed back to Texas. By agreement, the Texas-bound brothers carried the family gold with them. What they didn't use for purchasing land and livestock they were to bury in a secure location near the homestead. John and Lew Casner agreed to arrive at the ranch within two years.

Along the way, the two Casner brothers purchased sheep from various Indian herders they encountered in New Mexico, and by the time they arrived at the canyon they had accumulated a handsome herd.

The brothers found a suitable location deep in Palo Duro Canyon near the headwaters of the Red River. The two bachelors built a one-story sod and log cabin, hired a young Navajo to tend their sheep, and eventually built a large ranching operation.

While they were getting the sheep ranch started, the brothers selected a spot not far from their cabin in which to bury the family wealth. Near a stunted tree, within sight of the cabin, they dug a hole about three feet deep and placed into it a wooden trunk filled with gold coins. They covered the hole and laid a large flat rock across the top.

One afternoon, a small band of men rode into the canyon and up to the Casner home. The leader of the party was Sostenes Archiveque, an outlaw known for raiding, robbing, and killing in and around the many small settlements along the banks of the Rio Grande in New Mexico. So vicious was this outlaw that several communities banded together and eventually succeeded in chasing him from the area. In search of new places to plunder, Archiveque wandered into Palo Duro Canyon.

Archiveque had heard stories about the two Americans who lived in the canyon raising sheep. It was widely rumored that the men had buried a fortune in gold on their ranch, and the prospect of an easy robbery was appealing.

Archiveque despised Americans and killed them at every opportunity. It was said that his parents were killed by Americans when he was a very young child and that he had harbored intense hatred for whites ever since. Archiveque reportedly had slain at least twenty-three Americans at the time he rode into the Casner settlement.

Archiveque's band of outlaws was a scruffy-looking bunch of killers and men of small conscience. With them rode a young Mexican boy they had kidnapped from the small village of Tascosa only three days earlier. The boy was forced to set up camp, tend the horses, and do the cooking and cleaning when the outlaws stopped for the night. Archiveque told the frightened youngster that if he ever tried to escape, he would be shot.

As the band of outlaws rode up to the cabin, the Casner brothers walked out to greet them. Seeming friendly, Archiveque asked permission to hunt in the area. His men, he explained, were low on provisions, and they would like to add some venison to their food supplies.

The Casners gave their consent, gave Archiveque directions to a suitable location for hunting, and then asked the Mexican to join them for dinner that evening. During the meal, Archiveque invited the brothers to accompany him on the next day's hunt.

The next morning, Archiveque, two of his men, and one of the Casner brothers rode into the deeper reaches of Palo Duro canyon in search of deer. The other brother remained near the cabin to perform some chores.

The hunting party, on reaching a dense thicket of brush through which wound a narrow trail, rode into it single file. Casner was in the lead with Archiveque just behind him. Halfway through the thicket, Archiveque drew his revolver, spurred his horse close to the sheep rancher, and shot him in the head. After rifling his pockets and taking a watch and a few coins, Archiveque and his men rode back to the cabin.

The brother suspected something might be wrong when he saw the men returning so early and without his brother. Archiveque said there had been an unfortunate accident and that he had ridden back to summon help. While Casner was saddling his horse, Archiveque approached from behind and shot him through the head.

Archiveque ordered the captive Mexican boy to ride out to where the sheep were grazing and kill the Navajo herder. The boy agreed, knowing he would be shot if he refused, but once out of sight of the outlaw, he warned the herder, told him what had happened to the brothers, and then spurred his horse to Tascosa where he reported the killings to an old Indian sheepherder named Colas Martínez.

In the meantime, Archiveque tore the Casner home apart searching for the cache of gold coins. Finding nothing, he searched around the yard, dug a few holes in some promising locations, but had no luck. Archiveque decided to return to Tascosa.

Several residents who had been told by Colas Martínez of the depredations at the Casner ranch organized themselves and waited for an opportune moment. Eventually, they cornered the outlaw and shot him to death.

About a week after the killing of the Casner brothers, Leigh Dyer, brother-in-law of the famous cattle rancher Charles Goodnight, and J.T. Hughes, Goodnight's trail boss, rode by the Casner ranch. The Goodnight Ranch was in another part of the canyon, and the Casners were rarely seen. As the two cowboys rode through the canyon, they saw Casner sheep everywhere but could find no sign of a herder. On arriving at the low log and sod house, they discovered the body of one of the brothers, still lying where he had been shot and killed by Archiveque. A few hours later, they found the body of the other brother lying along the narrow trail in the thicket.

Dyer and Hughes rode back to the Goodnight Ranch and told their boss of the murders. Goodnight decided to ride over and see the sheep ranch for himself. Goodnight was appalled at the senseless murders of the two men. He searched both bodies and the cabin but found no indication of other family members. For several months thereafter, whenever Goodnight was in a city which had a newspaper, he would tell the story of the killings to a reporter and ask the newspaper to carry it in the hope that relatives of the dead men might be found.

At the time, John Casner and his son Lew were working a gold claim near Silver City, New Mexico, with two partners named Bell and Berry. Neither Casner could read.

One day, the younger Casner went into Silver City to purchase some supplies for the camp. Some of his goods were wrapped in a newspaper which coincidentally carried the stories of the killings in Palo Duro Canyon. When young Casner returned to camp, he unwrapped the merchandise and threw the newspaper away. Partner Berry picked up the paper and, seated on a rock after dinner that night, began to read aloud the contents. John Casner, stunned, recognized the description of the property and realized that the murdered men were his sons.

The next day, Casner, his son, and their partners abandoned the mining operation, packed their horses and mules, and departed for Palo Duro Canyon.

There they met Charles Goodnight and explained their relationship to the two dead men. Goodnight, convinced of their identity, took the men to the sheep ranch.

Casner knew that his sons had buried nearly $20,000 in gold coins somewhere near their home in the canyon. For several days, the men searched the area for a likely location but found nothing.

Having heard the story of the bandit Archiveque and his role in the killing of his sons, John Casner was developing an intense hatred for all Mexicans. He confessed his feelings to rancher Goodnight and swore that he would kill all the Mexicans in the area. Goodnight advised Casner of the folly of this notion and told him to take it easy. He told him that Mexican–American relationships in this part of the country were fragile at best, and that he must not go off half-cocked. The advice was lost on Casner.

One morning the following week, Casner and his son rode into Tascosa and, in a fit of hatred and poor judgment, killed Colas Martínez. They were unaware that Martínez was an Indian and not a Mexican. They were also unaware that it was largely because of Martínez that Archiveque, the man who killed his sons, was subsequently killed in Tascosa.

His hate at a boiling point, Casner hung Martínez's wife from a tree by her thumbs and threatened to kill her if she did not reveal the location of the buried gold coins, of which she had no knowledge whatsoever. Finally, they cut her down and rode away, never to be seen again.

The story of the buried Casner fortune in Palo Duro Canyon is still told throughout the Texas Panhandle, and though the canyon is now a state park, treasure hunters from around the country continue to search the area around the old Casner homestead hoping to find the lost cache of gold coins that have lain buried in the ground for well over a hundred years.

Silver Ledge in the Panhandle

Between the end of the Civil War and the turn of the century, the Texas Panhandle changed greatly. As settlers came and established large cattle ranches and farms, the native people were seen as nuisance and threat. The great herds of buffalo and the clans of the Comanche tribe were threatened with extinction.

The buffalo had provided a way of life for the Comanches and other plains tribes, but the animals were displaced by white settlers in favor of domestic cattle and butchered by the thousands by white hunters. Encounters between the profit-minded buffalo hunters and the Indians were common and usually violent.

Sometime in the 1870s, a small band of hide hunters were working the areas where Dickens, Kent, King, and Stonewall Counties come together in the southeastern Panhandle. They had seen few buffalo during the previous few days and hoped to find a herd large enough for them to fill their wagons with choice hides which they would sell for a nice profit in San Antonio.

As the party crested a low rise in the prairie, they surprised a band of Comanches coming up the other side. Shots were fired, and the buffalo hunters wheeled their horses and wagons around and rode for cover in a ravine.

In the scanty shelter of a jumble of rocks at the bottom of the ravine, the hunters made a defensive stand, firing at the Indians who rode back and forth on a nearby ridge, occasionally shooting back at the whites. The skirmish went on all afternoon, and the Comanches ran out of bullets. They shot arrows into the cluster of hunters hiding in the rocks, seriously wounding two of them.

As evening approached, the leader of the buffalo hunters took note that they were running low on bullets and ordered the men not to shoot unless they had a sure target. A quick inventory of ammunition suggested they could scarcely withstand another charge from the Indians.

All night, the men cowered among the poor protection of the rocks. No one slept for anticipating another attack from the Comanches at any moment. When morning arrived, there was no sign of the Indians, and one of the buffalo hunters climbed to the top of a ridge to see if he could spot any of them.

He looked for half an hour, saw no Indians, and felt sure they had left, at least for awhile. From the ridge, he scouted out the best route to use in quitting this dangerous country. The hunter reported his findings, and the men mounted their horses and wagons and left the area.

As anxious as they were to be far away, the hunters traveled slowly. The narrow, twisting trail in the small canyons made passage difficult for the hide wagons, and the men were being careful to make as little noise as possible. By sundown, they had gone only a few miles. They made camp and spent another sleepless night.

The next morning, there was still no sign of the Indians, and once again, a member of the party climbed a hill. After signaling that all was clear, the man examined the terrain to see which direction they needed to travel. As he was noting landmarks, he also noticed that the hill on which he stood was a peculiar reddish color, suggesting mineralization of some kind. Years later as he recalled his experiences, the buffalo hunter always referred to the hill as Red Mountain.

With the news that the Indians were nowhere near, the men built a fire and cooked some breakfast—it was the first solid meal they had eaten in two days. As buffalo ribs seared on the fire, one of the hunters grabbed several canteens and went to a nearby spring to fill them. At the spring and its clear pool, the hunter dropped to the grass and took several long gulps of the refreshing water. He sat up, and as he was wiping his lips on his sleeve, he spied a thin ledge of black rock on the opposite wall of the canyon.

Curious, the hunter knocked a piece of the rock from the ledge and examined it. It was unusually heavy, and when he cut into it with his skinning knife, he discovered it was quite soft and malleable. Convinced he had found a seam of lead, he called to his fellow hunters.

The discovery was celebrated by the men. Building a small fire near the ledge, they melted the metal and poured it into bullet molds. Within two hours, they had replenished their supply of ammunition and felt a bit more confident about traveling in dangerous Indian country.

Around noon, the party rode away from the ravine and the red hill. At Brady in McCulloch County a few days later, the hunters divided the hides and went their separate ways.

One of the hunters, whose name has been lost to history, sold his share of the hides, gathered up his few belongings, and journeyed to Mason, a full day's ride to the south, where he lived for many years with relatives.

A few years after coming to Mason, the buffalo hunter was to go deer hunting with his brother-in-law. Collecting his gear, he came across a pouch of the bullets he and his companions had fashioned of the soft dark rock from the Panhandle ravine. He divided up the bullets and gave half to his brother-in-law. When the brother-in-law saw them, he took one and scratched into it with his thumbnail. He examined several others and, to the the buffalo hunter's amazement, pronounced them to be pure silver!

When the hunter told the story of their escape from the Comanches and the discovery of the ledge of dark rock, it became clear to him that he and his companions had accidentally discovered a rich outcrop of silver.

The more the hunter thought about it, the more he decided he should go back to the Panhandle and claim the fortune he knew lay at the base of Red Mountain. Because he was a poor man, though, it was several years before he was able to return to the Panhandle.

On finally arriving in Stonewall County, the buffalo hunter, now an old man, was confused about landmarks and claimed the country had changed so much in his absence, he was unable to recognize anything. Indeed, several large cattle ranches had become established in the region, and the great herds of buffalo were gone.

The hunter knew if he could only find the low red hill near which he and his companions camped years earlier, he would be able to locate the silver ledge.

For months, the old man wandered the region searching for familiar landmarks. Because he was running out of money, he eventually took a job on an area ranch and pursued his search when he could.

The old man and the young son of the owner of the ranch grew close, and the old man often recounted his adventures with the Indians for the lad. He also told the boy the story of the discovery of the silver, taking care to describe the landmarks as he remembered them. As old men often do, the ex-buffalo hunter retold the story so many times that the boy soon knew it by heart.

One day as the old man was preparing another expedition into the hills in search of the elusive red mountain, his heart gave out and he died. The story of the fortune in silver he believed to exist somewhere in the nearby hills remained with the boy as he grew to manhood, and as an adult, he often wondered what his chances of finding the mysterious ledge might be.

As a grown man raising a family and running a ranch, the one-time friend of the buffalo hunter who used to sit and listen to the old man's stories of the lost silver ledge decided to search for it himself.

Like the old hunter's, the rancher's forays into the hills were infrequent, but he felt he was getting close to the ledge. Once, while he was driving along a seldom-used dirt road in the extreme southeastern part of Dickens County, he discovered a low hill of a peculiar reddish color. Stopping at a nearby ranch, he asked the owner about the hill and about roads that might lead to it. The ranch owner said it was known locally as Round Mountain, but some folks referred to it as Red Mountain because of the iron in the layers of sandstone that make up most of the landform. The rancher also told his visitor that on a previous trip to the hill, he found some strange mineralization at its base but could not identify it. He said it was a kind of black rock that had a lot of heft to it. When asked to describe it a bit more, the rancher said he had brought back a piece of it once and was using it as a doorstop in the ranch house kitchen. He took his visitor in and showed him the rock.

The visitor took out his knife and cut a piece from the soft rock, molding it easily into a ball with his fingertips. The rock was pure silver!

When the visitor got to the red mountain, he found it fenced off, and learned it was now the property of one of the large cattle ranches in the area. Trespassing was strictly forbidden. He tried several times, unsuccessfully, to speak to the ranch owner about obtaining mineral rights. Eventually, the obligations of managing his own ranch took him away, and he never renewed his search.

Today this region is part of the huge Pitchfork Ranch. It is likely that an occasional ranch hand in search of stray cattle has ridden along the base of the red mountain near the small spring and passed with a few yards of the ledge of dark rock, oblivious to being within spitting distance of a fortune in silver.

Incan Treasure on the Salt Fork

One of the most incredible tales of buried treasure to come out of Texas is that of a legendary Incan hoard said to be buried near the Salt Fork of the Brazos River in Stonewall County. The treasure, estimated variously by experts to be worth between $60 million and $100 million, reportedly consists of the equivalent of forty mule-loads of gold and silver bullion, jewelry, emeralds as large as goose eggs, and several jewel-encrusted golden Incan icons. Researchers also suggest that one of the first Bibles ever to arrive in the western hemisphere may be in the cache.

While the presumed location of this lost treasure is in the arid Panhandle region of Texas, the tale began more than 450 years ago and three thousand miles away in the mountains of South America, in what is now the country of Peru and was then the homeland of the mighty Incas.

In February of 1531, Spanish soldier-explorer Francisco Pizarro arrived with a convoy of three galleons at the port of Callao in western Peru. Accompanying Pizarro was a contingent of soldiers, a priest, and twenty-seven horses. Under orders from the Spanish monarch, Pizarro was to explore the country in search of precious metals, which he was to mine or confiscate and ship back to Spain.

Pizarro had established in several military campaigns a reputation for ruthlessness, and the king of Spain thought him well-suited for the job of conquering portions of South America and seizing the continent's wealth.

After several months of making plans and stocking up on supplies and equipment, Pizarro led a force of 170 armor-clad Spanish soldiers into the forested foothills of southeastern Peru. They attacked and destroyed every village they came to, indiscriminately killing men, women, and children and seizing food and livestock. In several weeks of working their way through the rugged countryside, they wreaked uncommon human misery and failed to locate any significant amounts of precious metals.

The Spaniards arrived at the large Indian village of Cotapampas in the foothills of the Andes. Here they found gold and jewels in large quantities, but the greedy Pizarro wanted more. Using torture, he learned from the people of Cotapampas that the Inca stronghold of Cajamarca, six hundred miles to the northwest, was a storehouse of gold, silver, and emeralds. Pizarro forced several of the Cotapampas Indians to guide his force to Cajamarca.

On November 15, 1532, Pizarro and his men took up positions around the gates to Cajamarca, a city of some two thousand people. Sending his priest and an interpreter to the gate, he demanded an audience with the Inca ruler, Atahualpa. When Atahualpa appeared, the priest told him he must accept at once the Christian teachings of the Spaniards, acknowledge the king of Spain as the ruler of the world, lay down his arms, and turn over his entire fortune to Pizarro. When these demands were interpreted, the priest proffered the Bible to Atahualpa. The implication was that if the Inca leader accepted the book, he agreed to the demands.

Incensed, Atahualpa hurled the Bible onto the ground and retreated into his city.

Pizarro sounded the battle cry, and the Spaniards crashed through the gates of Cajamarca, initiating one of the bloodiest slaughters in the history of South America. In spite of being vastly outnumbered, the far better armed and trained Spaniards subdued the city after brisk fighting. Hundreds of Incan warriors were slain and hundreds more taken prisoner, only to be horribly tortured and killed before the week was over.

The ruler Atahualpa himself was taken prisoner and brought before Pizarro in chains. Pizarro ordered runners sent throughout the countryside to tell the people that if they were to save the life of their ruler, they must bring all of their gold and silver as ransom. Journals kept by Pizarro's secretary said this ransom was to be of sufficient quantity to fill three rooms, each twenty-two feet by seventeen feet, to a point as high as a man can reach. The Incas were given two months to comply and save their leader.

Because Atahualpa was a beloved man among the Incas, the citizens lost little time in collecting the gold and silver and bringing it to the Spaniards. One of Athualpa's captains, a soldier named Rumiani, was sent northward to Quito with a small party of warriors and a pack train of llamas to retrieve the gold and silver of that city. When Rumiani did not return at the appointed time, Pizarro sent a military detail of a dozen men to ascertain the reason for delay and hasten the delivery of the wealth. Along with this platoon of armed soldiers, Pizarro also sent the priest and his interpreter.

As a result of misunderstandings and misinformation, the citizens of Quito refused to allow Rumiani to take their gold. Fighting broke out and was still raging when the Spanish soldiers arrived several days later.

When the rioting was finally quelled, the llamas were loaded with gold, silver, and gems, and arrangements were made to return to Cajamarca. The Spanish captain commanding the expedition, however, began to cast greedy eyes upon the great fortune being packed onto the animals and decided to escape with it himself. Taking into his confidence only six of the soldiers who accompanied him, the captain explained his plans.

Instead of returning to Peru, they would travel north with this huge fortune, far from the land of the Incas and into the new and wild country he had heard about from the Indians. He wanted to get so far away that Pizarro would not consider pursuit.

The captain sent one fully loaded pack train on its way to Cajamarca, accompanied by the six soldiers who were not a part of his plans. He ordered them to tell Pizarro that the second pack train would follow in a few days. The captain waited until the pack train was well along on the trail toward Cajamarca before he ordered the second one onto the trail to the north. In addition to his six confederates, the captain enlisted several of the Incas to accompany them and tend the llamas. With this renegade group traveled the priest, an unwilling participant in the theft and desertion. The priest walked at the rear of the rich caravan, clutching his Bible close to his breast.

Meanwhile, in spite of having received the entire ransom he had demanded, Pizarro had Atahualpa strangled in front of his subjects. He and his troops then moved on, sacking every city they came to and adding to the tremendous store of wealth he would eventually send back to Spain. Pizarro was so occupied with his own military activities that he apparently gave little thought to the desertions of several of his soldiers and the priest. In any event, he made no attempt to follow and apprehend them.

No one knows how long the escaping soldiers followed the prehistoric trade route which wound through mountains and valleys, coastlines and deserts, up through Central America and Mexico and into the unexplored country of Texas. Along the way, the party encountered many friendly Indians, obtaining from them food and directions. They journeyed through regions of extreme drought and others where monsoon-like rains fell for days at a time. They suffered hardship, disease, and starvation, but they endured. Their fear that they might be pursued by the relentless Pizarro kept them ever on the trail, ever alert, and always heading northward into unknown country where, with their stolen wealth, they hoped to establish their own kingdom.

During the entire journey, the captain compiled a map, continually recording their progress. The map was a large piece of rawhide, and inscriptions were burned into it with coals from the campfire.

One day, untold months after its departure from Quito, the pack train arrived in what is often referred to as the Double Mountain country of Stonewall County, a reference to the most prominent landmark in the vicinity. Double Mountain is between the present day city of Aspermont and the Double Mountain Fork of the Brazos River.

The Spanish soldiers saw that they were being watched and followed by Indians. Nervous and not knowing what to expect, they stayed close together and kept a vigilant eye on the landscape.

Traveling north of Double Mountain for another day, the party decided to make camp and rest the men and animals. They stopped, it is believed, on the banks of the Salt Fork of the Brazos River. The Spanish captain, fearing an attack by the Indians, decided to unload the llamas and bury the treasure close by. When it was safe to do so, he said, they would retrieve the wealth and continue their journey.

The leader assigned his men to dig twenty-one holes, each quite deep. Into these holes was placed the treasure from the pack animals. As the holes were being filled, the priest placed his Bible, carefully wrapped and tied in a piece of soft leather, on top of one of the piles of treasure. Once the holes were filled, the animals were led back and forth across the ground, covering any signs of recent excavation. That evening as he sat by the campfire, the captain recorded information about the location of the treasure on the rawhide map. For several days, the party of Spaniards and their Incan helpers remained in this area resting up and making plans to head for a more agreeable climate.

It is not known what became of the group of deserters; the record of their journey seems to end at their campground on the Salt Fork of the Brazos. Some researchers believe the group fell prey to Indian attack not long after burying the treasure. All were apparently killed, leaving no one who could identify the location of the fabulous cache. Evidence for this conclusion includes the discovery of several skeletons and Spanish artifacts such as armor, weapons, and tools unearthed in the late 1800s near Kiowa Peak in the northeastern part of Stonewall County. The rawhide map was not found among the artifacts. It did, however, appear many years later.

After the Civil War, this part of Texas began to attract settlers who came to ranch. As more and more people moved in, the legend of the buried Incan treasure in Stonewall County was often on the lips of residents. There were a few half-hearted attempts to locate the cache, but none of them ever amounted to anything.

Interest in the Incan treasure was revived in 1876 with the arrival of an elderly Spaniard. Having come to Stonewall County in a fine carriage pulled by two stately horses, the old fellow quietly bought up several parcels of land along the Salt Fork. The settlers who lived in the area presumed the old man was going to establish a ranch, but after several weeks, it was clear that ranching was not on his mind. The old fellow moved into a tent on his property, rarely came into a settlement to purchase goods, and behaved somewhat mysteriously. On the few occasions he was seen by townspeople, the old Spaniard always carried what appeared to be a large piece of rawhide, a map which he studied constantly.

After living there several months, the Spaniard disappeared as suddenly as he had arrived. Several neighboring ranchers entered his property to look around. They found the tent the Spaniard had lived in for many months, now torn to rags by the incessantly blowing wind. Here and there were abandoned tools—shovels, picks, and buckets. And not far from the tent site, the men discovered ten freshly dug holes! The ranchers reported the holes were very deep and had obviously contained crates and packs.

No one knows what became of the Spaniard. Did he in fact recover a large portion of the buried Incan treasure? All the evidence suggests he did. And what of the remaining eleven holes as described on the rawhide map by the Spanish captain more than 450 years ago?

While several old timers in Stonewall County claim to know where the ten excavations were made, flash floods, sandstorms,and erosion have long since obliterated any sign of them.

Shortly after the turn of the century, another Spaniard arrived in Stonewall County, this one much younger than the first and also carrying an ancient map inscribed on rawhide. Though it can probably never be proven, many believed the rawhide map was the same one brought a quarter of a century earlier by the previous Spanish visitor, and there was also speculation that the newcomer was a relative, perhaps a son.

After spending several days near the property originally purchased by the first Spaniard, the more recent visitor went to the nearest town, bought tools and provisions, and hired four men to do some digging for him.

The men hired as laborers reported that they followed the Spaniard around the area of the Salt Fork for several days while he checked landmarks, constantly referring to an old rawhide map. Finally, he gave the workers instructions on where to dig.

The diggers soon excavated four skeletons in the first hole—but nothing more. At several other locations, the men dug holes nearly fifteen feet deep and found nothing.

On the day the diggers were to be paid, the Spaniard told them he had insufficient funds but would cut them in on a share of the gold he believed they would eventually uncover. After several days of digging in the hot summer sun of West Texas and finding nothing, the workers grew hostile and threatened the Spaniard. That evening, the terrified European gathered up the rawhide map and a few other possessions and fled, never to be seen again.

Many believe the young Spaniard was at the correct site of the buried Incan treasure cache and that he had holes dug in the proper locations. The consensus is that he simply dug into the holes that had already been excavated by the earlier Spaniard.

In 1909, an elderly, overweight man with considerable mining experience arrived in the Double Mountain area. Like the two Spaniards before him, he had a map—this one, however, was on parchment, not rawhide. The man's name was David Arnold, and he quietly explored the region looking for certain landmarks.

After several months, Arnold made an amazing discovery: he found a rock near the confluence of the Double Mountain Fork and the Salt Fork that appeared to have a map inscribed on its surface!

The map contained several markings that suggested a Spanish origin, and nearby were found several Spanish relics. Because of the radial symmetry associated with a series of lines extending from a central point, the rock has become known locally as the "Spider Rock" and is linked to the caching of the Incan treasure. Over the years, other "Spider Rocks" have been discovered in this region. Several researchers continue to work on interpreting the markings, but at this writing, the rocks have remained undeciphered.

In his late seventies, Arnold's physical infirmities, along with a troublesome divorce he was going through, prevented him from continuing his search for the treasure, and he eventually had to abandon his quest.

About three years later, a former wolf hunter from Rotan came to the region to search for the treasure. His name was Walter Leach, and like Arnold, he concentrated his activities near the confluence of the Salt and Double Mountain Forks of the Brazos. Though the multi-million dollar Incan hoard eluded him, Leach did discover a cache of gold that eventually netted him $12,000. Along with the gold were buried several Spanish artifacts. Over the next several months, Leach discovered other smaller caches of gold and silver, but none as large as the first.

In 1920, a well-heeled Illinois farmer named Frank D. Olmstead somehow came into possession of the rawhide map. Olmstead claimed he bought it and another from a Spanish priest during a vacation in California. Olmstead began to study everything he could find concerning the lost Incan treasure. Captivated by the tale and fascinated by the possibility of uncovering the cache he knew lay near the Salt Fork, Olmstead moved there, purchased several hundred acres of land, and undertook a search for the treasure that lasted twenty-eight years!

Olmstead once told a confidant he would gladly give up the entire Incan treasure if he could only get his hands on the Bible he believed to be buried with the hoard. How Olmstead learned about the existence of the Bible remains a mystery.

Olmstead eventually purchased the same plot of land owned by the first Spaniard. Thousands of holes were dug, but Olmstead never found anything. He died at sixty-three and is buried on his property. In death, he may repose atop one of the rich caches he sought for so long during his life.

The treasure of the Incas, at least a portion of it, is still hidden somewhere in the rough and broken country of Stonewall County near the Salt Fork of the Brazos River. Only the ghosts of the Spaniards know where.

North Texas

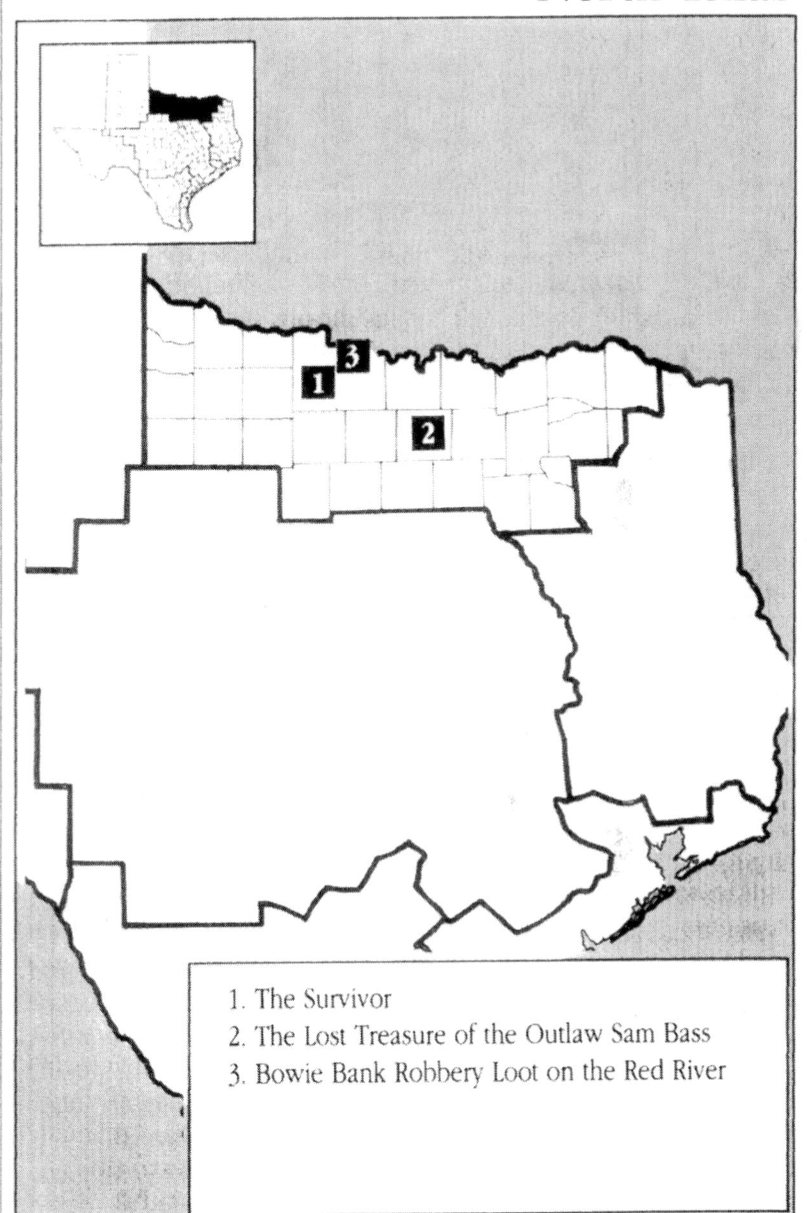

3
1
2
1. The Survivor
2. The Lost Treasure of the Outlaw Sam Bass
3. Bowie Bank Robbery Loot on the Red River

The Survivor

The old California Trail cut across a great expanse of North Texas. Travelers from the east seeking to start a new life in California or some place along the way west followed the trail in great numbers. The wagon trains made their way across the dry country, dodging Indians and linking major water holes with rutted tracks. Many families succeeded in the arduous journey to the fertile fields and rich mines of the west. Others were not so fortunate.

One such train was having a relatively easy time of crossing North Texas along the old trail. In spite of the distances between water holes and the boredom of the endless prairie, this party of seventeen wagons was making good time. Then tragedy struck.

Just as the wagon train entered what would become Clay County, a war party of Comanches appeared on a low rise to the north. The travelers stared in awe at the painted horsemen, and the Indians charged the unprepared party, firing rifles and loosing arrows into the wagons.

The wagon master shouted for the drivers to circle up to defend themselves against the charging Comanches. As the men whipped the mules and oxen and tried to guide the wagons into position, they could not fire back at the Indians, and several of them were killed during the attack. The wagons were finally arranged in a ragged circle, and the panicked members of the party scrambled for their guns and sought cover. The Indians regrouped on the low rise and readied for another attack.

The second assault was more devastating than the first, and several more members of the wagon train were killed. This time, the Comanches penetrated the circle of wagons and inflicted heavy damage on the defenders. The Indians suffered losses, too, and retreated again to the low rise.

One of the white men stayed in a wagon, wedged between two large trunks. He hid and prayed. After the second attack, he ventured a look from under the canvas and watched as the Comanches fled to the rise.

Taking advantage of this lull in the fighting, the man left the wagon and skulked around the circle of defense, ignoring commands from the others to seize a weapon and take up a position. When he saw that no one was looking, he dashed between two wagons and fled across the prairie toward the south. None of the party saw him leave, and he was out of sight of the Comanches who were regrouping on the far side of the wagon train.

The man had run hard for no more than three minutes when he heard the cries of the Indians and the rifle fire from the train. He flung himself into a nearby depression.

From here he could see the third and final attack on the wagon train. He watched through the tall prairie grass as the Indians killed and scalped every member of the party. They killed all the oxen as well and secured the horses and mules. The wagon train was looted and set afire, and as the dark smoke rose in the Texas sky, the Comanches loaded their booty onto the mules and prepared to leave.

The man feared they would come in his direction. Having just witnessed the murder and scalping of his companions, he closed his eyes and began again to pray. When he finally found the courage to open his eyes, the Comanches were riding toward the rise from which they had launched their attack. The last of the warriors disappeared over the low rise, and the man, the only survivor of the wagon train, lay alone on the bleak prairie.

For the remainder of that day and the entire night, the survivor lay in the shallow depression, afraid to move.

When the sun rose the next morning, he found himself desperately thirsty. The fear of the previous day had lessened not at all. He scanned the surrounding prairie and saw nothing but grass in all directions. Several hundred yards to the north, the embers of what was left of the wagon train were dark on the plain.

As he looked around his hiding place, he saw it was an old buffalo wallow where the great shaggy beasts flung themselves into the dust and rolled around, seeking relief from parasites. Knowing that buffalo wallows sometimes yielded water if one dug deep enough, the survivor went to the lowest point of the depression and began to scoop out the dirt with his bare hands.

With the first two scoops, the survivor noticed a grainy, pebbly texture to the otherwise soft prairie soil. Looking more closely, he found several nuggets that glinted in the sun. He rubbed them clean. They were pure gold!

He continued to dig, eventually retrieving enough nuggets to fill all the pockets in his pants and coat.

Among the nuggets, he also found pieces of rotted leather and deduced they were the remains of pouches in which the gold was once carried. The survivor surmised that someone had buried the gold in this spot, no doubt intending to return for it.

At a depth of two feet, he found water and slaked his thirst. Heartened by both wealth and water, the man cast one final glance in the direction in which the Comanches were last seen, abandoned his hiding place, and began to walk south in hope of finding a settlement.

After about an hour, the weight of the gold in his pockets became too much for him, so he emptied a few small handfuls of the nuggets into a shallow hole he dug into the prairie soil. He searched for some rocks with which to mark the site but found none. Finally, he twisted and tied together several bunches of the tough prairie grass in order to mark the spot. He went on.

After another two hours or so, he emptied more of the heavy nuggets into another cache, marking the location as he had the first.

On he traveled, and by the end of the day, his hunger and thirst and the weight of the gold fatigued him to the point he simply dropped to the ground and fell asleep.

The next morning, he buried more of the gold and proceeded southward. Walking was considerably more difficult than the day before, and he began to wonder if he would live through the day. Twice more before the sun set, he lightened his load by emptying some of the contents of his pockets into another prairie cache.

On the third day, he stumbled into a tiny settlement along the bank of a narrow river. He was delirious and near death from hunger, thirst, and exposure.

Crying tears of joy at the sight of fellow humans, the survivor related the tragedy of the wagon train massacre and of his own cowardice. He told them of his discovery of the gold at the bottom of the buffalo wallow and of his flight across the prairie. He reached into his pockets to show them the gold and was surprised to discover he had discarded all of it save for a small handful of nuggets.

The residents of the small community nursed the survivor back to health and eventually found him a job with a local merchant.

For the next several years, he tried to retrace his steps across the vast North Texas prairie in search of the gold caches he left along the path of his flight, but he was never able to locate them. Others who knew his story also searched the prairies for years but with no success.

Disappointed and in poor health, the survivor eventually left the small community to settle in Wichita Falls, where he died a few months later.

The Lost Treasure of the Outlaw Sam Bass

The legendary Sam Bass was one of many notorious outlaws that operated out of Texas in the last century. Following a series of daring holdups and the accumulation of thousands of dollars in gold coins and jewelry, the famed outlaw buried his wealth in Denton County, where it supposedly remains today.

Like those of many famous outlaws, the story of Sam Bass mixes legend with fact, but there are enough facts about his escapades to validate his reputation as a cunning and efficient outlaw and a clever and successful robber.

Bass was born in Indiana in 1851. Orphaned early, he was passed from relative to relative and forced to work long days on the various farms on which he lived.

At eighteen, Bass determined to escape from the toil and grind of farm work. He dreamt nightly of traveling to Texas and becoming a cowboy. One day he packed what few belongings he possessed and struck out for the Lone Star State.

Bass arrived in Denton County in 1870, having turned nineteen on his journey. A strapping young man not afraid of hard work, Bass found a job on a local ranch and learned horsemanship and livestock-handling. At first, he was thrilled at riding and roping and leading the life of a working cowboy, but the daily tedium of tending cattle soon bored him and he sought more creative outlets.

Bass found work with a Denton freight company owned and operated by the county sheriff. He began to haul freight throughout North Texas and as a result came to know the countryside, the trails, and the people. A charming young man, Bass readily made friends.

During this time, Bass developed an intense interest in horse racing and often squandered his earnings betting on races. In time, he acquired his own racing mare and began to travel the countryside betting his horse against others. His travels took him into Oklahoma and parts of eastern Texas, and after several months of racing and betting, Bass's winnings were handsome.

Joel Collins, a friend of Bass's from his cowboying days, talked the future outlaw into investing his winnings in a herd of cattle. The two men combined their herds and arranged to drive them to Dodge City, Kansas, where they expected to sell them and make a keen profit.

By the time the young cattlemen arrived at Dodge City, the market had taken a turn for the worse. They were discouraged and undecided as to what to do. Killing time in a Dodge City tavern one afternoon, they learned that top dollar was being paid for beef in Deadwood, Dakota Territory. Deadwood was the center of a huge gold mining boom, and the citizens were paying high prices for fresh meat. Several weeks later, the herd arrived at Deadwood where it was sold for a decent profit.

After many months on the trail, and with their pockets heavy with money, Bass and Collins paid off their drovers and began what turned into a long and expensive celebration. Their night on the town included a great deal of drinking and gambling, and before the sun rose the next morning, the two men had managed to spend just about all they'd earned from the sale of their cattle. Disgusted with themselves, Bass and Collins began to wonder how they were going to get back to Texas.

After several fruitless days looking for work in Deadwood, they were broke. In desperation, they decided to rob a stagecoach. Enlisting the help of three other men who were also down on their luck, they spent the next six weeks holding up stagecoaches near Deadwood.

Robbing the stages was easy, and before long they sought greater challenges. Bass considered robbing the bank at Deadwood, but decided security was too strong. The gang drifted south looking for easier prey. They occasionally robbed stagecoaches and travelers along the way and eventually arrived at Big Springs, Nebraska.

The Union Pacific Railroad ran through Big Springs, and the gang rode toward the train station. Hiding in a grove of trees just beyond the building, the outlaws watched as the eastbound train pulled in. When the crew was distracted with filling the water tanks, the outlaws struck.

Wearing masks, they rode up to the train crew, leveled their revolvers at them, and forced them to open the locked door of the express car. To their delight, the outlaws found a payroll trunk containing three thousand freshly minted twenty-dollar gold pieces, each bearing a date of 1877.

After loading the gold onto the horses, the outlaws systematically robbed all the passengers. This done, the gang mounted up and rode off into the night.

After they had ridden for almost an hour, the outlaws halted and divided the loot. Bass suggested they split up to confuse any pursuers, and within minutes, each of the bandits was riding off in a different direction.

Bass returned to Texas with his saddlebags filled with gold coins and jewelry. On arriving back in Denton, he learned that his friend Collins had been captured by law enforcement officials in Nebraska and subsequently shot and killed. Twenty-five thousand dollars' worth of gold coins and jewelry were found in Collins's saddlebags and returned to the railroad.

Because of the newness of the coins and the fact that each bore an 1877 date, Bass feared they would be easy to identify. He decided it would be foolish to begin spending them, so he cached them, intending to return for them in the future when detection would be less likely.

Bass established a hideout at Cove Hollow, a relatively isolated area surrounded by dense forest and brush about thirty miles from the town of Denton. Within days, Bass organized another gang that robbed stagecoaches in the area. As the stage companies grew more wary and added more guards, Bass turned to trains. In six weeks, he and his new gang robbed four of them near Denton. Bass was recognized during one of the train robberies, and his image soon appeared on wanted posters throughout the area.

Many believed that after Bass committed a robbery, he took his share of the loot to his Cove Hollow hideout and added it to the cache of gold coins. His fortune grew.

Slowly, but most surely, the Texas Rangers were closing in on Sam Bass. As the noose tightened, he abandoned the Denton area and led his band of outlaws south to Central Texas.

Bass made preparations to rob the Williamson County Bank at the settlement of Round Rock, and one of his gang members, a man named James Murphey, tipped off the Texas Rangers. The Rangers arrived in Round Rock one day ahead of Bass and set a trap. As the outlaw and two of his men rode up to the bank, at least two dozen Rangers opened fire, and a brief gun battle ensued. One member of the gang was killed in the first burst of gunfire. Bass was seriously wounded and fell from his horse. He managed to climb back onto his mount and flee. The third member of the gang escaped unharmed.

The Texas Rangers tracked the wounded and bleeding Bass the next morning and found him seated under a big cottonwood tree, bleeding to death. They tied him to a horse and returned him to Round Rock, where he died on his twenty-seventh birthday.

People began to wonder about the vast wealth they believed Sam Bass had accumulated. Some who were in sympathy with Bass claimed he had given most of the money to the poor and needy. (This Robin-Hood image often attributed to Bass had some basis in fact, for he was given to helping the underprivileged.) There were also people who believed Bass was a ruthless outlaw who gambled away all the money he stole.

But most people believed Bass hid his wealth in a shallow cave near Cove Hollow. This may be true, or partly true: there is evidence that Bass may have split up his treasure and cached portions of it in different places around North Texas.

Around the turn of the century, a farmer named Henry Chapman found what many believe was part of the Sam Bass treasure. Chapman owned a small farm near Springtown in Williamson County. One day as he was riding through the woods between Clear Fork Creek and Salt Creek, Chapman's mule began acting contrary. The farmer dismounted to check the girth on the balky animal, and as he was tightening it, he noticed a low mound of dirt just off the trail. At first he believed it to be a grave, but closer examination revealed it was not.

Chapman dug into the mound and was surprised to discover a bushel-sized wooden box filled to the top with gold and silver coins. All the gold coins bore the date 1877!

Except for these, none of the rest of Bass's 1877 gold coins ever appeared in circulation, supporting the belief that the rest of his treasure is still buried intact somewhere in North Texas, awaiting discovery by some fortunate treasure hunter.

Bowie Bank Robbery Loot on the Red River

Early one late spring morning in 1894, four strangers rode into Bowie, Texas, a growing community in Montague County. With studied casualness, the men lingered near the town's only bank until the manager arrived to unlock the doors. After exchanging greetings, the four men followed the manager into the building, giving him the impression they wished to conduct some business.

The strangers pulled out their pistols and ordered the manager to fill several canvas sacks with money. He did as he was told. Before he was done, though, two bank employees arrived for work and surprised the robbers. One of the bandits panicked and began firing at the newcomers. Grabbing the few bags that had been filled with coins and cash, the robbers fled from the bank to their horses, which were tied nearby. During the getaway, the group was fired upon by several citizens and one resident was killed in the crossfire. The robbers escaped unharmed. Within the hour, a posse was organized and left in pursuit of the bandits.

The bank manager later reported the bandits absconded with a total of $10,000 in twenty-dollar gold pieces along with $18,000 in other currency. The bank robbers headed north, apparently to Rock Crossing, an important ford on the Red River. After crossing the river, they would be in the lawless environs of Indian Territory. The Territory, as it was called, was perceived as a relatively safe haven by criminals because of the paucity of law enforcement there. Only weeks earlier, though, a small detachment of federal marshals had been ordered to Comanche, twenty-five miles north of the river. The marshals were assigned by Judge Isaac Parker, the famous "Hanging Judge" of Fort Smith, Arkansas, to subdue the lawlessness pervading the region.

The bank robbers got an unwelcome surprise at Rock Crossing. The Red River was well above flood stage as a result of recent spring rains and impossible to cross.

Unaware of any pursuit by the Bowie townspeople, the outlaws decided to make camp in a grove of cottonwoods on the south bank of the river and try to cross in the morning when they believed the water level would be lower. That evening, the men split the currency from the robbery but left the gold coins tied up in the canvas sacks.

In the meantime, the posse was doggedly following the trail of the outlaws in spite of the rains.

When the city marshal at Bowie realized the outlaws were headed north, he notified the federal marshals he knew to be stationed in Indian Territory. Since Rock Crossing was the only safe place to cross the Red River for several miles in either direction, the federal marshals went there.

When the outlaws awoke around daybreak, they saw the level of the river had gone down some. They were preparing to cross when one of them saw the posse coming from the south. They saddled up and grabbed their gear. Fearing the weight of the sacks of gold coins might jeopardize their escape across the river, one of them quickly scooped out a shallow hole by a large tree near the campsite, deposited the sacks, and hastily covered it.

With the posse close enough to shoot at them, the four outlaws took off, plunged into the river, and made for the other side. Though the water level was lower than the day before, the crossing was difficult and dangerous. On several occasions, horses and men went under and resurfaced farther downstream. Finally the exhausted and frightened outlaws made it across. Climbing the low bank to a nearby clump of trees, they were greeted by the federal marshals who had just arrived. The four bank robbers meekly surrendered to the lawmen.

Most of the paper money was recovered from the saddlebags, but none of the twenty-dollar gold pieces were there. The four bandits denied any knowledge of the gold.

One of the marshals, a man named Palmore, was to deliver the captives to Fort Smith, where they would stand trial for the robbery of the First National Bank of Bowie and the murder of one citizen. Palmore, accompanied by one other marshal, escorted the robbers on the long journey to Fort Smith, then known among the lawless as "Hell on the Border." Along the way, Palmore and the oldest of the robbers engaged in friendly conversation and often played cards together by the campfire in the evenings. On several occasions, Palmore questioned the outlaw about the twenty-dollar gold pieces the outlaws were known to have taken from the bank, but the bandit would just smile and wink at the lawman.

Weeks later, the four appeared in the courtroom of Judge Parker, the renowned hanging judge. The trial was quick and the judgment swift—all four were found guilty and sentenced to hang.

On the day set for hanging, Palmore and several other deputies were ordered to escort the outlaws to the gallows just outside the courthouse. The four were noticeably pale, both from spending several weeks in the dark chamber of a jail cell underneath the courthouse and from the fear of dying on the gallows. Palmore helped each of the manacled outlaws up the thirteen steps to the gallows floor. The last one in line, his card-playing associate, turned to him and winked once again.

The hangman placed a black hood over the head of each condemned man before securing a noose around his neck. As the second prisoner was pushed forward to receive his hood, the older outlaw leaned toward Palmore, who was standing near him, and whispered that the gold coins were buried beneath a large tree near where the outlaws camped the night before they were caught. Again the outlaw winked at Palmore, and then he stepped forward to meet his fate.

It was many months before the marshal could return to the area of the outlaws' campsite. Because Palmore never actually saw the outlaw camp (he never crossed the river the day of the capture), he was unsure of its exact location. The area was a well-used ford and stopping place, and there were many campsites in the timber on the high bank on the Texas side of the river.

Palmore believed the outlaw's story and was convinced the cache of gold coins could be found. Selecting a likely campsite, Palmore dug around the bases of several trees. Finding nothing, he moved to another campsite and made more excavations. His searches proved unsuccessful.

Because of his obligations as marshal, Palmore couldn't stay long. He returned on several other occasions to search for the coins, but success continued to elude him.

Some researchers believe the gold coin cache is located close to the confluence of the Red River and the Little Wichita River in a grove of cottonwoods. In recent years, however, some of the woods near the river have been cleared to extend cropland, and it is possible that the coin cache may now lie a few inches below the surface of a cotton field. Some have suggested that if the coins were buried close to the riverbank, erosion over the ensuing years may have uncovered the cache and washed it to the bottom of the river. Others note that the river was at flood stage when the coins were buried, and the outlaws' campsite was likely far back from the normal riverbank.

Whatever the case, there is no evidence that the gold coins taken in the Bowie bank robbery have ever been found. Today, this cache would be worth several times its original value.

Central Texas

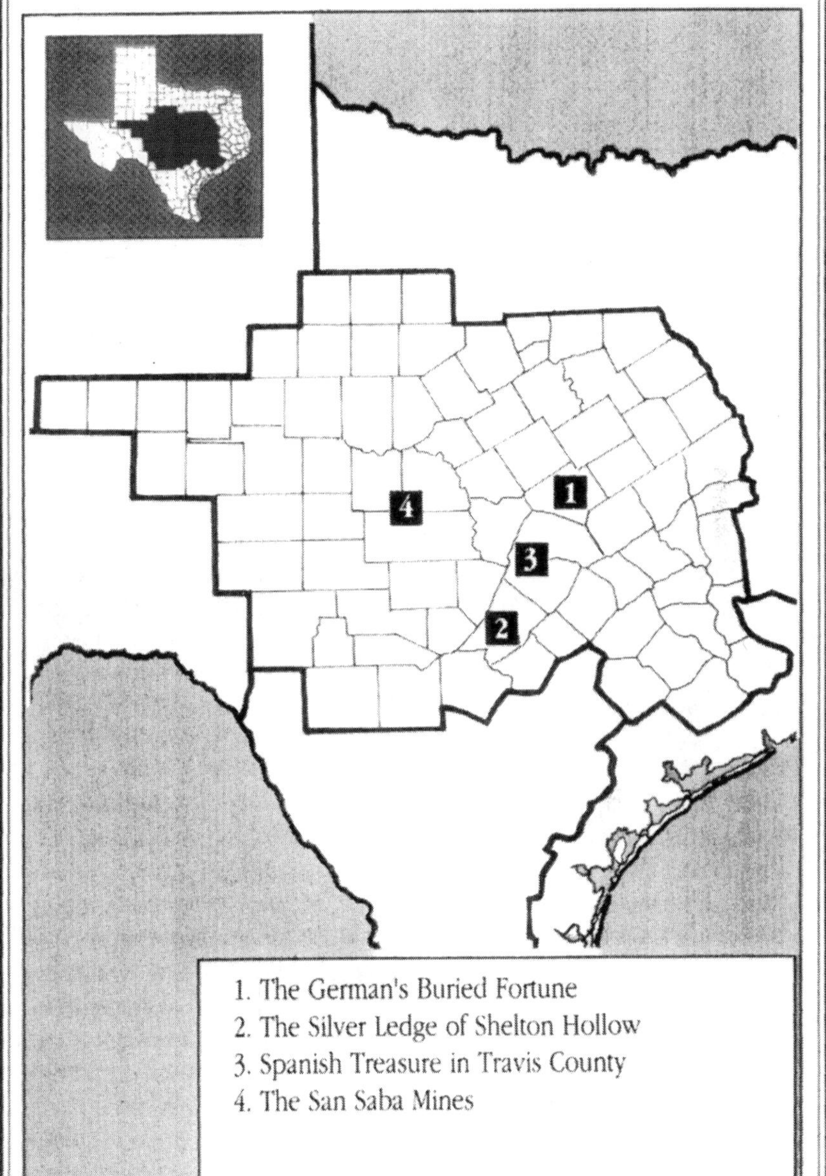
1
2
3
4
1. The German's Buried Fortune
2. The Silver Ledge of Shelton Hollow
3. Spanish Treasure in Travis County
4. The San Saba Mines

The German's Buried Fortune

Karl Steinheimer was born on the outskirts of Speyer, Germany, in the spring of 1793. He was a boisterous, energetic youth with a sense of adventure that often got him into trouble. Karl did not readily take to working in the fields with his parents; he preferred to play in the nearby woods. And when it came to schooling, Karl resisted all attempts to get him to read and write.

Karl's free and independent spirit led him to run away from home at the tender age of eleven. Making his way to the North Sea, he found work aboard a freighting vessel. He became an expert seaman, and several years as a deck-hand on the open ocean toughened the youngster.

Having docked in South Africa one summer, Karl hired on as a deckhand with a sailing vessel that turned out to be a pirate ship. The life of raiding and pillaging appealed to Karl's lust for adventure, and before long, he became as proficient at piracy as he was at swabbing decks.

Steinheimer sailed the Atlantic for years, working alongside fellow cutthroats attacking and robbing ships and piling up vast stores of gold, jewels, and other treasures. He eventually commanded his own ship, and for many years thereafter, the name Steinheimer was known and feared in Atlantic sea lanes.

Once when his ship needed repairs and supplies, he put in at New Orleans. While his men worked to make the ship seaworthy, Steinheimer partook of the pleasures of the city.

The debonair Steinheimer met and fell in love with Marie Nicole Savoy, a Frenchwoman who charmed the pirate to the core of his being. The pirate, when he wished to be, was equally charming, and his nights were pleasurably spent with Marie Nicole.

Before sailing, Steinheimer promised Marie Nicole he would stay in contact with her. Though it was difficult to do in his line of work, Steinheimer sent letters to her two or three times a year. Marie Nicole replied to each and encouraged Steinheimer's return to the Crescent City.

The years of robbing, raiding, and murder began to take a toll on Steinheimer, now in his forties. He grew tired of piracy. His restlessness led to disagreements with his partners, and he decided to leave the sea and take up mining in the mountains of Mexico.

Steinheimer had heard of the rich gold and silver mines in the Sierra Madres and was determined to try his hand there. By the time the ex-pirate was forty-five years old, he had become a successful miner, daily taking small fortunes in gold and silver from the rock matrix of the Sierra Madres.

In March, 1838, Steinheimer got a letter from Marie Nicole telling him she had moved with her family to St. Louis. The letter brought a rush of memories. After some days of pondering his life and future, he decided to abandon the mining operation, pack up his wealth, and go to St. Louis to marry Marie Nicole. He sent word to her of his intentions.

With the help of two faithful workers, Steinheimer loaded ten burros with leather sacks and large clay jars filled with gold coins. Accompanied by the two men, Steinheimer began the long journey. He intended to travel overland to Matamoros, where the Rio Grande entered the Gulf of Mexico. From there, he would book passage to New Orleans and on up the Mississippi River to St. Louis.

After several weeks of uneventful travel, he arrived in Matamoros. While purchasing supplies, Steinheimer learned of the defeat of Mexican General Santa Anna two years earlier at the Battle of San Jacinto. He also learned that the Mexicans were secretly making plans to retake Texas by creating an Indian uprising. The Indians, aided by the Mexican army, would attack and kill settlers, thus paving the way for the Mexicans to move in and reclaim the land they believed rightfully belonged to them.

In Matamoros, Steinheimer met with Manuel Flores, a spirited officer in the Mexican army who was organizing a company of men to travel to Nacogdoches, where they would begin their campaign against the Texans. Concerned about his gold, Steinheimer decided to bypass New Orleans and travel in the company of the Mexican soldiers.

The party traveled several weeks through the humid, mosquito-infested lowlands along the coastline. Finally they arrived at the Colorado River, where they learned that General Burleson was rapidly approaching with two companies of heavily armed troops.

That night, as the company of Mexican soldiers prepared camp, Steinheimer decided to leave the soldiers and go on north. By dawn, Steinheimer and his two men had managed to drive the pack train about twenty miles.

Over the next few days, Steinheimer lost his bearings and instead of going northeast toward St. Louis, he traveled northwest.

Meanwhile, Flores and his company of soldiers eluded Burleson until they came to a point southeast of Austin where they met a detachment led by Lt. James O. Rice. A battle ensued on May 14, and Flores and most of his soldiers were killed. The few survivors fled to Mexico, and the plans to retake Texas were thwarted.

Steinheimer continued across the Texas prairie. One evening, his party arrived at the confluence of three streams. Weary of travel and longing to be with Marie Nicole, Steinheimer decided to bury his fortune and return for it later. The three men dug a shallow trench, placed in it the leather sacks and clay pots of gold, and then refilled it.

Those who have researched Steinheimer's journey believe the place is where the Lampasas, Leon, and Nolan Rivers come together near the present-day city of Temple.

Steinheimer rewarded his men for their devotion with several handfuls of gold each. Before they left, Steinheimer hammered a seven-inch iron spike into a nearby oak tree to help identify the site when he returned.

Steinheimer, relieved of his burden, decided to go back to the Colorado River, build a raft, and float to the Gulf. He would go through New Orleans to St. Louis, as he'd planned.

Toward the evening of the second day since hiding the gold, Steinheimer and his two men arrived at a place he referred to as a "bunch of knobs on the prairie." Along Steinheimer's route south from the confluence of the three rivers, this site could only be an area between Elgin and Lexington, some twenty miles north of the Colorado River. There they were attacked by Indians.

His men were killed immediately, and Steinheimer was badly wounded. The German gathered the gold coins he had paid the men and sought refuge atop one of the knobs. As the Indians searched for him, he dug a small hole and buried the coins.

Steinheimer stayed hidden from the Indians. Eventually they left, and Steinheimer slowly made his way to the Colorado River. At the bank of the river, he met and joined a party of travelers going downstream.

Steinheimer's wounds festered, and it was obvious he would not live much longer. He wrote a letter to Marie Nicole relating the events of the previous few days. He described in as much detail as he could the location of his treasure and the cache of coins atop the knob. He also sketched a crude map on the back of the letter.

Steinheimer begged Marie Nicole to wait three months for him. He told her that if he did not arrive in that time, she could presume he was dead and take on the responsibility of claiming his buried treasure.

Three months passed, and Steinheimer did not appear in St. Louis. History does not record what happened to him, and it is assumed he perished during his journey and was buried somewhere on the coastal plain.

In September of that year, Marie Nicole enlisted the aid of family members in searching for the treasure Steinheimer said he had buried. Using his map, the search party was able to locate the three knobs outside of Lexington. For several days, they searched and dug there, but they did not find the small cache of gold coins hidden by the German.

They went to the confluence of the Lampasas, Leon, and Nolan Rivers and spent several days looking for the large oak tree with an iron spike embedded in it. The group eventually gave up and returned to St. Louis.

This tale, like many others of lost and buried treasure, would have ended at this point were it not for two events.

One day in the late 1870s, a party of three Mexicans arrived at the town of McBride, a small settlement near where the three rivers come together. Keeping to themselves, the Mexicans established a modest camp by one of the rivers. For several days, they searched up and down the bank, stopping occasionally to dig. Their activities attracted the attention of several McBride residents who turned out to observe the Mexicans at their labors. A few old-timers recalled the story of Steinheimer's buried gold and concluded that the Mexicans were searching for the old pirate's treasure.

One of the residents got to know the Mexicans, who told him this was indeed what they were looking for. After several more days of searching, though, the Mexicans left.

Twenty years later, A.C. Urvin, a young man who lived at McBride, decided to visit his father some thirty-five miles southwest in Burnet County. Urvin was traveling on foot, and after he'd crossed the Lampasas River, he sat on a low stump to put his socks and boots back on. When he got up, Urvin noticed the "stump" was the top of an old clay jar extending just above the level of the grassy bank. Urvin pried off the lid and discovered it was filled nearly to the top with gold coins!

He stuffed his pockets with several handfuls, carefully replaced the lid, and covered up the jar with soil and brush. With the cache well hidden, he went on to his father's house.

That evening, Urvin dined with his father and a neighbor, John Hart, from nearby Florence. Urvin said nothing about his find, and later that night went alone to another room to examine his coins. There, his father and Hart found him.

At first they accused him of stealing the coins, but Urvin finally told them about the buried clay jar. The next day, Urvin and his brother, returned to the bank of the Lampasas River and uncovered the buried vessel. They filled two *morrales* with gold coins, reburied the pot, and returned to their father's house.

The story of the gold coins spread, and a rumor started that young Urvin was involved in the theft of the coins from a Florence man named Atkinson. Atkinson claimed he possessed a fortune in ancient Spanish coins but was unable correctly to identify any of them.

Urvin was cleared of any wrongdoing and soon afterward left the region. No one knows if he took all the coins from the clay jar or if he was aware that there were other containers of treasure buried years earlier by Steinheimer.

Many believe the remaining coins still lie buried somewhere along the south bank of the Lampasas River. Treasure hunters convinced of it are now even further frustrated because the Lampasas, Leon, and Nolan Rivers have been damned to form Belton Lake and Stillhouse Hollow Lake, submerging the presumed site of Steinheimer's buried fortune.

The Silver Ledge of Shelton Hollow

It was just a few years after the Civil War, and people interested in taming new lands were coming to the sparsely populated regions of central Texas. The small settlements of Wimberly and Hugo in Hays County were far from the action of the War, but residents were nevertheless happy for things to return to normal.

L.J. Dailey homesteaded a rocky piece of land a few miles southwest of Wimberly. Dailey, like most farmers in that part of Texas, worked desperately hard to grow a crop and raise a few head of livestock on the dry, grudging Texas soil.

Dailey was bit of a loner, unmarried, and seemed happy working his small holding by himself. His one passion was his pack of hounds. He was known for the fine dogs he raised, and when he wasn't working, he could be found running them in pursuit of wolf, deer, or fox.

Dailey and other men from Wimberly, Hugo, and San Marcos would gather from time to time with their hound dogs just outside of Hugo on a ridge known as the Devil's Backbone. As soon as the sun touched the horizon, the men turned the hounds loose to pick up a scent. Before long, one of the dogs would find a trail, and off they would all run in baying chase.

On one autumn night, the dogs took off across the ridge after a wolf, with the men running along behind. The chase led into a narrow canyon known locally as Shelton Hollow, one of the many deeply eroded canyons that drain into the Blanco River. The wolf crossed the canyon about half a mile north of the river.

There were no trails, and both dogs and men scrambled down the steep sides of the canyon. The terrain was rough, and several men slid, tearing their clothes and getting a little skinned up.

The chase crossed the narrow floor of Shelton Hollow and went up the steep wall on the other side. Dailey, looking for a shortcut, lagged behind. Picking a route, he climbed the wall, using outcrops for hand- and foot-holds.

During the climb, Dailey grabbed a rock, and a piece of it broke loose in his hand. Off balance, he tumbled several yards to the bottom of the canyon, still clutching the rock.

He wasn't hurt, and he got up and scanned the slope for an easier route. As he did, he noticed that the piece of rock he still held was quite heavy for its size. It was too dark to tell what kind it might be, so he stuffed it into his coat pocket and continued to search for a way to the top of the ridge.

The chase went on toward the Blanco River, up and down ridges and through narrow hollows. Near the river, the men and dogs gave up the hunt, exhausted. They rested and then headed back to Hugo, arriving at daybreak.

After a leisurely breakfast and an hour or so of spirited conversation about the hunt, the group eventually broke up. Each man gathered up his dogs and headed for home. Dailey had forgotten all about the rock in his coat pocket.

About a week later, Dailey put on his coat to ward off the autumn chill as he went about his farm chores. He felt the weight of the rock in the pocket, reached in, pulled it out, and examined it. To his amazement, the rock appeared to be embedded with generous deposits of high-grade silver ore!

Dailey asked several other people to examine the rock, including the Wimberley blacksmith, Greenberry Ezell.

Ezell was reputed to be knowledgeable about gold and silver and occasionally traded in them. Ezell and the others all agreed that the mineral in the rock was silver and that it was almost pure.

Dailey tried to remember exactly where he had gotten it. He recalled he had grabbed it from a ledge on the north side of Shelton Hollow as he tried to climb to the ridge. The next day, he went to the hollow and tried to find the exact spot along the bluff where he had fallen.

In the daylight, the terrain looked much rougher than it had that dark night the week before. The hollow was long and the walls were steep and high, and Dailey could not find the place the rock came from. He searched all day.

Over the next few months, Dailey returned to Shelton Hollow many times to look for the lost ledge of silver, but he came back empty-handed each time.

One day, when Dailey was visiting the blacksmith, Ezell, in Wimberley, and telling him of his bad luck, Ezell told him an interesting and curious tale.

When Ezell had first arrived in Wimberley several years before the War Between the States, an Indian came to his blacksmith shop. The Indian had two small sacks filled with high-grade silver that he wanted fashioned into bullets. Ezell did so and charged the Indian a fair price for his efforts. The Indian came many times during the next few years, always alone, and always with the two small sacks filled with silver nuggets.

As Ezell and the Indian grew friendly, the blacksmith tried to discover the origin of the silver. At first, the Indian refused to speak about it, but as he grew to trust the blacksmith, he was less cautious about his secret.

One day, the Indian arrived with the usual two sacks of silver and request for bullets. As Ezell melted the ore and poured it into bullet molds, the Indian said he was preparing to make a long journey to visit relatives far to the north, and before he left, he wanted to tell the blacksmith the location of the silver.

In a drawn out, singsong manner, the Indian gave Ezell directions to the ore. He told him to begin at Moon Peak, a low mountain just south of the Blanco River and about five miles southwest of Wimberly. From Moon Peak, he was to travel due east, crossing three canyons and four ridges, descend to the bottom of the fourth canyon, and search the north wall for a thin outcrop of the silver. The Indian told Ezell his people had been digging silver from the outcrop for many generations.

One day a few weeks after the Indian's last visit, Ezell closed his blacksmith shop and traveled muleback to Moon Peak. From the peak, he followed the directions provided by the Indian, eventually descending into the fourth canyon. For the remainder of that day and most of the next, Ezell searched for the outcrop of silver but was never able to locate it. He finally gave up and returned to Wimberly.

The fourth canyon from Moon Peak, Ezell told Dailey, was Shelton Hollow.

Spanish Treasure in Travis County

In the middle of the eighteenth century, the Spanish operated a rich gold mine in what is now called Dagger Hollow, about fifteen miles northwest of Austin, in Travis County. The ore was melted and formed into ingots at a smelter near a small creek that trickled along the bottom of the canyon and eventually fed into the Colorado River. When approximately eighty burro-loads of the ingots had accumulated, they were packed into specially made leather saddlebags, loaded onto the beasts of burden, and transported nearly a thousand miles to the treasury at Mexico City. The mine yielded millions of dollars worth of the ore for many years, and it seemed as though the thick vein of gold would continue forever.

As the 1760s neared an end, however, the miners began to experience threats from the area Indians, who resented the intrusion of the Spaniards into their hunting grounds. Hunting parties of miners were attacked, and Indians were often seen watching the workers from vantage points high on the canyon rim.

The person charged with overseeing the operations of the gold mine was named Maturo. Early in 1770, Maturo decided that the threat of Indian attack was great enough to warrant closing down the mine for a time and withdrawing the men, livestock, and gold to Mexico. In the tradition of Spanish miners in the New World, the entrance to the shaft was sealed and camouflaged. They would load the ingots and equipment onto the burros.

As a result of an Indian raid on the herd the night before, however, the Spaniards found themselves in possession of only a dozen burros. Realizing they would have to leave the largest part of their accumulated gold, Maturo ordered the miners to cache a total of seventy-five burro-loads of ingots in a nearby cave, which, like the mine, was sealed up and covered to resemble the surrounding area. When this was done, Maturo chose two flat pieces of limestone and scratched several symbols onto them with an iron bar, symbols that indicated the location of the mine and the ingots. He carried the stones to the mouth of the hollow and hid them under a bush. The miners destroyed the smelter, loaded the remaining gold onto eight burros, and fled the canyon. Maturo and his young son, Benito, rode together on one of the spare animals.

The Spaniards had no sooner left the hollow than they began to see Indian signs. As they rode a trail beside the Colorado River, they occasionally spotted Indians watching them from distant hills. About two dozen were following the column at a distance of about two hundred yards.

After nearly a full day of slow and nervous traveling, Maturo called a halt near what is now Barton Springs in Austin. Men and animals were exhausted and needed rest and water. While some of the miners cooked, others removed the heavy loads from the burros and stacked them near the campfire. The burros were turned out to graze. Maturo, worried by the constant threat of Indian attack, posted guards. Thinking the camp relatively secure, Maturo and his son went down to the spring to fill buckets with water. There they found moccasin tracks so fresh they must have been made only seconds before they arrived. And there were dozens of them.

Fearing imminent attack by the Indians, Maturo rushed back to camp to warn his fellows. The men erected a rude circular fortification of rocks and tree limbs, and into this poor defense they herded the burros and stacked their equipment. Near the center of the barricade, Maturo had his men dig a large hole in which they placed the eight burro-loads of gold ingots. As his son Benito watched, Maturo chose a flat rock and once again scratched directions to the mine and cache in Dagger Hollow. He laid the stone across the pile of gold ingots. Once the hole was filled, the site was covered with grass and debris to resemble the surrounding countryside. For the third time, Maturo chose a flat rock and scratched several cryptic symbols onto it with his iron bar. He wedged it into the crotch of a nearby cedar tree to serve as a marker should the party have to abandon the site and return at a later date.

As the sun began to set and shadows stretched across the encampment, the miners could see Indians in the dim distance as they surrounded the fortification. Maturo took Benito to the rear of the barricade and arranged a hiding place for him between some rocks and tree limbs. He cautioned the lad not to leave the shelter until he was certain the Indians were gone.

Maturo had just returned to his post near the eastern rim of the barricade when the Indians struck. The fight lasted nearly an hour and a half. The Indians shot hundreds of arrows into the fortification, killing and wounding many of the miners. The Spaniards, in turn, fired their muskets into the throng of howling attackers, likewise dispatching many of them. But the Spaniards were outnumbered ten to one, and the outcome of the battle was inevitable. When the miners' ammunition was gone, the Indians jumped the barricade and killed them one by one. The victims were scalped, their bodies looted and mutilated. When the Indians were done, they faded into the night.

Young Benito Maturo heard the terrible sounds of battle from his hiding place, and even when they ceased, he was afraid to leave the shelter. It was late morning the next day before he left his cramped hole.

All around lay the results of the carnage of the previous night. The stunned youngster walked away from the bloody battlefield and, with only the sun to guide him, undertook a long journey toward the southwest.

For days he walked, living on ripe cactus fruit and frogs he was able to catch. He found water in potholes and the occasional streams he had to cross. The boy stumbled onto a road headed in the general direction he wished to travel, and he followed it for several more days. He was overtaken by a small wagon train bound for Mexico City, and after hearing the ragged youngster's story, the travelers invited him to journey with them. Many weeks later, the party came to Mexico City. Benito was taken in by relatives.

As Benito Maturo grew up, he never forgot the experience of the Indian attack at the springs. When he was old enough to appreciate the value of gold, he recognized the wealth of ingots buried near the springs and in the cave at Dagger Hollow. He also realized he was the only person left in the world who knew the location of the cached gold.

Benito often dreamt of going back and recovering the treasure, but he was unable to do so. The few times there were chances to travel north, some turmoil in Texas or along the Rio Grande placed Mexican and Spanish travelers at risk. For a while, Mexico and Spain engaged in a war of independence, and the Indians who ranged throughout much of Texas were still a menace. When these threats died down, Mexico went to war with the United States, and then the Civil War kept Texans nervous for a number of years.

When the War Between the States came to an end, the danger that threatened much of Texas died down. Benito, now an old man who claimed 108 years, crossed the border and made his way to central Texas and to the springs, now called Barton, where he knew the treasure was hidden. Once Benito arrived at the flourishing town of Austin, he employed two men to guide him to the springs. He told the men the tale of the eight burro-loads of buried gold ingots and offered the entire amount to the guides. All

Benito wanted was the flat rock buried with the gold bars, the rock that contained the directions to the cache of the seventy-five burro loads hidden in Dagger Hollow.

When Benito and his guides finally arrived at Barton Springs, the old man was unable to recognize a single feature. He could not remember in which direction from the spring the fortification had been located. In addition, much of the region had grown up in brush and parts of it had washed out in deep gullies. Benito told the guides about the rock on which his father had carved several cryptic symbols. On the back page of an old Bible, Benito recreated the markings as he remembered them. Neither he nor the guides were able to locate the rock, and after six weeks of fruitless searching, the old man gave up and returned to Mexico, where he passed away a year later.

More time passed, and the area around Barton Springs attracted more and more settlers. One of them was a man named Hamlin who claimed a section of land near the springs on which he farmed and raised a few beef cattle. Hamlin had no family and was regarded by his neighbors as a poor farmer and not a little lazy. Hamlin's farm was ill-tended, and if it were not for hunting and the occasional sale of one of his cattle, Hamlin would have made hardly any living at all.

Whenever Hamlin shot a deer or butchered a cow, he would dig a pit on the spot and cook the animal at once. Then he'd load the cooked meat onto his rickety wagon, take it to Austin, and peddle it to customers on the streets.

An occasional visitor to the Hamlin farm was a man named Jarber. Jarber was interested in buying the Hamlin section and farming it himself. Jarber made Hamlin decent offers for the land several times but was always turned down. One day, however, Hamlin appeared interested and told Jarber he would like to consider it and would give him an answer after he butchered and cooked one of his cows.

Hamlin rode off in his creaky wagon toward the spring to perform his work.

That evening, Hamlin approached Jarber and told him he would trade his entire farm for Jarber's new Studebaker wagon and a pair of good mules. Jarber thought Hamlin had lost his mind and agreed to the offer before the farmer could withdraw it.

The next week, Jarber rode across most of the 640 acres. Near Barton Springs, he noticed a deep pit which had been dug into the ground. Jarber assumed it was where Hamlin had cooked his cows a few days earlier. He also noticed wagon tracks leading up to and away from the pit. He gave them no thought until several days later.

About a week later, Jarber began to think that the wagon tracks leading away from the pit were considerably deeper than those that led up to it. Assuming Hamlin had loaded the cooked beef onto the wagon, it still would not have been enough weight to cause tracks to sink into the soil like that. It also occurred to Jarber that he didn't remember seeing bones, hide, or other residue from a butchered cow in the area.

Out of curiosity, Jarber saddled his horse and rode back to examine the tracks and the pit more closely. He found the imprints of metal bars at the bottom of the pit, bars the size of gold ingots!

Jarber searched around the immediate area. He found an old cedar tree which contained a rock wedged into a crotch. With some difficulty, Jarber removed the rock and saw that it had some strange markings carved onto the surface. As it turned out, these markings were like those described and drawn by Benito Maturo several years earlier. This rock was still in the possession of the Jarber family as late as 1960.

And what became of Hamlin? The poor farmer who apparently quite by accident discovered the cache of gold ingots near Barton Spring while digging a cooking pit found himself suddenly very wealthy. Hamlin was seen several days later making a sizeable deposit in an Austin bank, but he disappeared shortly thereafter. Years later, it was learned that Hamlin moved to Oregon, purchased several sections of prime agricultural land, and became part owner of a bank!

And what of the other stone that was buried with the treasure at Barton Springs, the one with directions to the cache of seventy-five burro loads of gold ingots? It is likely that Hamlin, assuming he found it while removing the gold, did not recognize it for what it was and merely left it in the hole or nearby. Jarber was unaware of the existence of these directions until many years later.

Sometime in the 1940s, a boy hunting raccoons near the mouth of Dagger Hollow discovered two interesting flat limestone rocks lying on the ground. They were the rocks onto which Maturo had scratched directions to the mine and the cache and which he had hidden near the mouth of the hollow on leaving. The boy showed the rocks to others and found that at least one of the markings was a Spanish symbol for "treasure." Another series of markings on the rocks were identical to those drawn by Benito Maturo and identical to the ones on the rock Jarber found wedged into the cedar tree near Barton Springs.

It is believed that the cryptic markings are a code which identify the location of the seventy-five burro loads of gold ingots hidden deeper in Dagger Hollow. Many have tried to interpret the odd markings, and many others have combed the walls of Dagger Hollow searching for a likely cave or mine hidden behind a cover of debris. To date, no discovery has been made.

The cache of Spanish gold ingots would be worth an incredible fortune today.

The San Saba Mines

Few tales and legends of lost and hidden treasures in Texas are more enduring than those associated with the lost San Saba mines. First seen by white men in 1756, the rich silver mines of the San Saba region were apparently well known to area Indians for centuries, and Comanches and Apaches claimed to have regularly visited the region to extract the almost pure silver for making jewelry and ornaments and sometimes for trade.

The San Saba mines, also known as the Bowie mines, have been found and lost several times during the past two-and-a-half centuries, but interest in the allegedly very rich site has never flagged. As recently as the summer of 1990, a cache of silver bars, obviously smelted by a crude technique known to have been used in the area, were found buried on a ranch adjacent to the region where the lost San Saba mines are believe to exist.

Word of the mines came to light in 1756 during a military expedition headed up by Lieutenant-General Don Bernardo de Miranda. Miranda was sent from the village of San Fernando (now San Antonio) to the northwest to look for minerals and to assess the strength of the local Indians. After traveling for eight days and covering only ninety miles, the slow-moving expedition set up camp near Honey Creek, a southern tributary of the Llano River.

While men and horses rested, Miranda and several of his miners rode out to explore the region. Crossing the Llano River and venturing some fifteen to twenty miles north, Miranda and his men came upon the San Saba River and a low, red-colored hill. Curious, they explored the canyons and ravines extending from the hill and found a natural cavern in one of them. Lighting torches, Miranda and a few soldiers entered the cave and discovered several thick veins of silver.

Miranda returned to San Fernando and sent a dispatch to his commanding officers in Mexico City alerting them to the possibility of great riches in the hills to the northwest. As proof, Miranda sent several large chunks of rock containing representative samples of the ore.

Miranda's superiors were not as enthusiastic about the silver as was he. After considerable haggling and a commitment by Miranda to share in the costs, the Mexican government finally agreed to let the young officer take thirty men to the area, establish a presidio, and begin mining and smelting the silver. Unfortunately, the authorization to undertake this mission arrived several days after Miranda had been sent on another military expedition in East Texas near the Sabine River. Miranda was never heard from again, and the Mexican government's interest in the potentially rich mining enterprise faded.

As Miranda was trying to convince his superiors to construct and garrison a fort near the Llano and San Saba Rivers, a Mexican viceroy actually authorized the establishment of a mission for converting the warring Apaches and Comanches to Christianity. The mission was eventually located not far from the San Saba River.

Though it has never been verified, legend claims that the mission priests discovered an Indian silver mine almost immediately in the nearby hills and spent more time extracting and smelting ore than they did bringing salvation to the natives.

When the Mexican government learned of the successful mining operation, it ordered a force of one hundred soldiers to the mission to protect its interests. About this same time, the Comanches, resentful of the growing encroachment onto their traditional hunting grounds, attacked the mission and the soldiers with a war party of nearly two thousand Indians, killing everyone. As far as is known, the Mexican government never ventured into the region again to search for silver.

Over the years, ranchers, prospectors, sheepherders, and geologists have reported seeing the ruins of the old mission. Many expeditions have ventured out from this site into the surrounding hills to find the silver mines, but they remain elusive.

Sometime in the early 1830s, a man named Harp Perry, along with two friends and thirty-five Mexican laborers, opened and operated a silver mine in the area of the San Saba and Llano Rivers. The group also had some success in removing gold from the nearby rock matrix. Every three weeks, Perry and several of the Mexicans would lead a pack train of some ten to twelve burros to San Antonio, each burro carrying a load of silver bullion. In the city, Perry converted the silver to coin and made large deposits in several banks. Perry and his comrades are also believed to have buried several hundred pounds of silver bars in the area of the mines.

Perry and the others had built a crude smelter about a half mile from the complex of mines and hauled the raw ore to it on burros. The men poured the molten silver and gold into hollowed-out lengths of the cane that grew along the ravine bottoms. This process yielded ten- to twelve-inch–long bars of bullion.

During this time, travelers, settlers, and miners in this part of Texas were having serious trouble with bands of Comanches intent on driving the newcomers from the area. In 1834, a large war party of Comanches attacked the miners, killing all but Perry and two others. After hiding in a narrow rock niche for three days, Perry escaped from the area and made his way to Mexico. There, he married and lived comfortably on his wealth for many years.

In 1865, when Perry was an old man and had gone through most of his savings, he decided to return to the San Saba region to retrieve some of the gold and silver he and his companions had buried in the area of the mines. In particular, Perry wanted to recover the twelve hundred pounds of bullion cached on a high hill about a mile and a half north of the little smelter. Perry had marked the site well when he buried the treasure some thirty years earlier: it was seventy-five yards from a spring, and in a direct line between the spring and the cache was a large pin oak tree with a big rock plugged into a knothole. Nearby were the remains of an ancient smelter that pre-dated Perry's arrival in the area.

When Perry returned to the San Saba country, he was surprised at how much it had changed. Large ranches with great herds of cattle dominated the region and much of the land had been overgrazed. Flash floods had changed the courses of rivers and streams and the configurations of local drainage basins. Small towns and settlements existed where none were before. Perry had difficulty getting his bearings and eventually decided to employ a guide to help him find the treasure site again. Although the two men covered most of the country on horseback for several days, they were unable to return to the mines. Discouraged, Perry eventually took a job driving cattle to Oklahoma and was killed a short time later in an accident.

In 1878, a drifter named Medlin took a job herding sheep on a big ranch between the San Saba and Llano Rivers. Medlin often remained for days at a stretch alone with his herd in the rugged Central Texas limestone country, and it was during one such occasion that he accidentally discovered what may have been Harp Perry's mines.

After he had worked for the sheep rancher for about a year, Medlin was given charge of a large herd that grazed in what he called the "Llano Hills." There he chanced upon evidence of mining. The sheepherder found several sites that appeared to have been excavated and subsequently covered over. On a nearby hill not far from a spring, Medlin found the ruins of an old smelter and a pin oak tree with a large rock wedged into a knothole. Unaware of Perry's treasure cache, Medlin passed over the area.

The legends of the San Saba Mine and those of the colorful frontier character Jim Bowie have often overlapped. Bowie, renowned knife-fighter, adventurer, businessman, and one of the fallen heroes of the Alamo, may have discovered the San Saba mines and extracted a considerable amount of ore from them.

Traveling through Central Texas in search of adventure and new business enterprises, Bowie learned that the Lipan Apaches of the Central and West Texas plains often visited San Antonio, bringing with them leather pouches full of silver which they traded for goods, firearms, and ammunition. Bowie, eager to find the source of the Apaches' silver, made plans to contact the tribe's leaders.

Alerted to an impending visit to San Antonio by the Apaches, Bowie went there, bought an expensive rifle, and used it to cultivate the friendship of the Apache chief, a fierce warrior named Xolic. Having gained Xolic's confidence, Bowie left San Antonio with the Indians and began a long association with them as a member of the tribe. Living among them and fighting against enemy tribes, Bowie was soon regarded as a brother and included in their ceremonies. He learned the secrets of the sources of the Apaches' silver and began to make plans to acquire some for himself.

Bowie abandoned the Apaches as soon as he knew the location of the mines. He went to San Antonio to organize an expedition to mine the silver.

According to legend, Bowie established a camp at the site of the ruins of the old mission. With the help of a group of twenty miners, Bowie allegedly excavated a great deal of ore and made several large deposits in San Antonio banks.

Bowie was heard to comment several times that the mines from which his silver had been taken were previously worked by Spaniards.

At the end of the first month, Bowie's camp was attacked by Apaches believed to be members of Xolic's tribe. For nearly a week, the miners fought the Indians off, but so many of them suffered such serious wounds that Bowie was forced to abandon the area and return to San Antonio. Because the Indians throughout this part of Texas—Comanches, Apaches, Caddos, and Wacos—were continually attacking wagon trains, settlers, and miners, Bowie opted not to return to the San Saba until later. As he was making plans to mount another expedition, he was killed at the battle of the Alamo.

Though often reported to have been seen, the rich silver mines of the San Saba range remain hidden from those who would recover their treasures.

In 1852, a trader who occasionally sold goods to the Comanches between San Antonio and the Red River purchased a young female captive from the Indians. She was a Mexican who had been stolen from her family several years earlier during a raid on her family's *rancho* in the state of Coahuila, Mexico. On returning to San Antonio, the trader gave the woman her freedom, and she was dogged by several newspaper reporters who begged her for descriptions of her life with the savages.

The woman provided material for several issues of the local newspapers, and one of the tales she related concerned the gathering of silver near the San Saba River and making jewelry and ornaments from it.

The former captive claimed the Comanches camped on the site of the old mission while they went to the nearby mines and dug out the silver. She said that the Indians would leave the grounds of the old church, ride across the San Saba River and up Los Moros Creek. The women followed the braves and waited for them near the creek.

She said the Indians would be gone for less than an hour and return with several pouches filled with ore which they would give to the women to carry back to camp.

After a series of Indian raids on ranches near Lampasas, about twenty ranchers banded together and took up pursuit of the Comanches with the intention of recovering their stolen stock and punishing the malefactors. One member of the group was a young man named Adam Beasley, and it was during the pursuit of the Indians that he may have accidentally discovered the San Saba Mines.

The trail left by the fleeing Indians and the stolen cattle and horses was plain and easy to follow. The Comanches crossed the Colorado River and then turned northward toward the San Saba. After a full day of riding, the leader of the pursuing expedition ordered a halt, and the men set up a hasty camp.

When Beasley went to the picket line early the next morning, he discovered his horse had broken away. As the others were just rising from their bedrolls, Beasley began to search. Two hours later and several miles from the campground, he found his mount grazing at the bottom of a shallow ravine through which trickled a small spring.

Beasley caught up with the horse and was leading him back to the camp when he noticed the mouth of a cave in the wall of an adjacent ravine.

Beasley staked his horse and walked over to the cave. Finding the lure of the cavern irresistible, he pulled a bundle of grasses, twisted them together to form a crude torch which he lit, and entered the dark cave. About forty feet beyond the entrance, Beasley held the torch up against one wall and found it was thickly seamed with veins of pure silver. Scattered about the floor of the cave were old tools and timbers, evidence of some long-ago mining.

As his torch burned down, Beasley left the cave to find that his companions had been searching for him most of the morning. After being reprimanded for delaying the pursuit, he was ordered to mount up, and in a short time the group was once again following the trail of the Comanches.

Beasley kept the secret of the silver cave to himself. About a week later, the group went home and Beasley went back to work on the family ranch. Keeping a cattle ranch going interfered with his return to the cave of silver. When an opportunity to go search for the cave finally presented itself, news came that the area was thick with renegade Comanches. He decided not to go.

Several months later, Beasley moved to Tennessee, married, and settled in the foothills of the Appalachian Mountains for two years. While he farmed a fertile valley near Knoxville, Beasley found himself thinking constantly of the cave of silver on the San Saba and longing to return to take up the search.

He told his wife, and together the two traveled west to the area around San Saba, McCulloch, and Mason Counties, where they purchased a small ranch.

After getting a herd of cattle established, Beasley undertook to search for the cave. Although three years had passed since he saw the silver, he felt he would be able to ride directly to the cave with no trouble.

On the first day out, Beasley found the hilltop where he and the rest of the pursuit party had camped the night his horse broke away from the picket line. For several days, he rode out in different directions from the site in search of the cave of silver. Though he searched for nearly a week, Adam Beasley never found the cave.

It is likely that the San Saba mine, the Bowie mine, and Beasley's silver cave are the same. The only differences in the tales are the circumstances under which the rich mines are found. The similarities of location and content are remarkable.

Ever since Miranda formally reported the existence of silver in the region in 1756, hundreds, perhaps thousands, of treasure hunters, geologists, ranchers, prospectors, and adventurers have journeyed to the region of the San Saba in search of the elusive treasure caves.

If the mines have been found, the finder has not announced it.

South Texas Brush Country

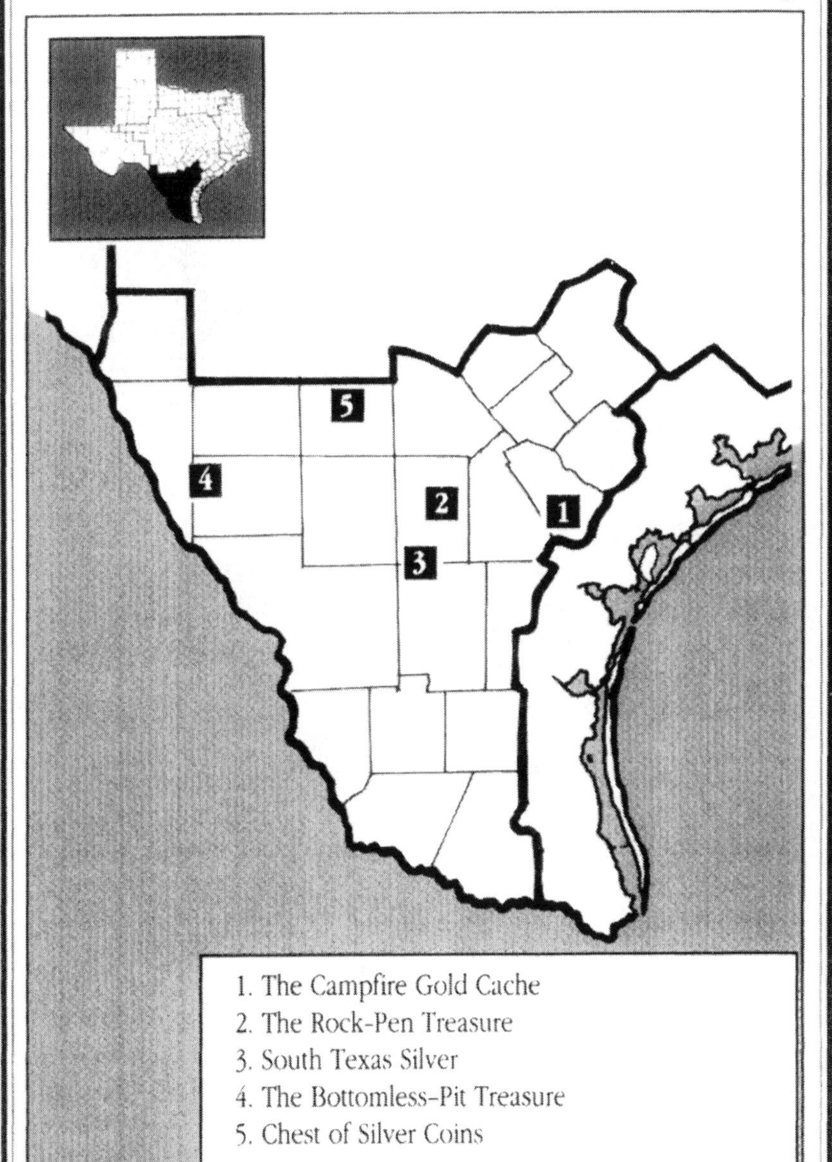

1. The Campfire Gold Cache
2. The Rock-Pen Treasure
3. South Texas Silver
4. The Bottomless-Pit Treasure
5. Chest of Silver Coins

The Campfire Gold Cache

A few years after the War Between the States, migrants from east of the Mississippi River began moving into Texas and settling from the humid Gulf Coast to the western edge of the semi-arid Edwards Plateau. Coastal cities such as Corpus Christi, Galveston, Houston, and Brownsville experienced impressive growth during this period as did many inland towns, such as San Antonio and Austin.

Men determined to pursue ranching for a living found rich soils and healthy grasses ideal for raising cattle and horses, and soon much of South Texas was carved up into large and prosperous ranches.

One rancher, who reportedly owned a twenty-six-thousand-acre cattle ranch near Brownsville, decided to buy a large herd of horses. Horses were in great demand, and a smart rancher and businessman anticipating the market for riding and breeding stock could make huge profits.

The rancher went to San Antonio, where he knew he would be able to buy as many unbroken range mustangs as he could handle. He also wished to invest in the economy of the burgeoning San Antonio area. To that end, he visited the Brownsville bank and withdrew $40,000 in gold. Packing the gold into saddlebags and loading it onto a pack mule, the rancher, alone, departed for the Alamo City. His route included a long stretch of seldom-used inland road that paralleled the coastline for nearly 140 miles.

The journey was to take the rancher due north to the town of Beeville. He was concerned about the first part of his trip, for the Brownsville road was dangerous—bandits frequented it, preying on unsuspecting travelers, taking their money and goods and sometimes killing them. From Beeville, however, the road which led northwest to San Antonio was well-traveled, and there would be little to fear from bandits.

On the afternoon of the first day of his journey, the rancher had a feeling he was being followed. From time to time, he stopped to scan the area he had just traveled. He saw nothing, but the feeling would not go away.

After three days of riding, the rancher came to the Nueces River, crossed it, and continued toward Beeville, now some thirty-five miles away. It was mid-afternoon, and he wanted to get as close to town as possible before stopping for the night. By the time the sun set, he had crossed into Bee County. He was tired and decided to make camp. Looking around in the fading light, he spotted two oak trees about fifty yards off the road to the west, and it was toward these he made his way.

Setting his horse and mule out to graze, the rancher contentedly prepared a meal and looked forward to arriving in Beeville in the morning, where he intended to rest up for a few days before going on to San Antonio.

As he went about his camp chores, the rancher could not rid himself of the feeling he was being followed. During the day, he had thought he heard faint sounds of a horse's hooves striking gravel. As he bustled about the camp, he sensed the presence of others nearby, and once, he thought he heard a horse whinny in the distance.

On a hunch, the rancher yanked the gold-filled packs from the mule, quickly dug a shallow hole between the two oak trees, and buried them. He built a small campfire on top of the cache and prepared his evening meal. In the morning, it would be a small matter to dig up the gold and be on his way, but for the night, he felt a need to be prepared for anything.

Having finished his dinner and cleaned and put away the gear, the rancher lit his pipe and reclined against the bole of one of the oak trees. He looked up from the flickering light of the low campfire to see two men riding toward him across the flat ground between the road and his camp, their guns raised.

Abandoning everything, the rancher leaped upon his horse and, riding bareback, tried to flee. He was overtaken and thrown from his horse. The newcomers told him they knew about the $40,000 in gold he was carrying and ordered him to turn it over to them immediately. The rancher denied he was carrying any money and invited the outlaws to search his camp.

The bandits returned with the rancher to the campsite, and while he watched, they searched through his belongings, scattering clothes and gear across the small clearing. Several times the bandits asked the rancher where he'd hidden the gold, but he revealed nothing, always claiming he was a poor man and possessed little of value.

Frustrated, the bandits told him they would keep him prisoner until he decided to reveal the location of his gold. Tying his hands behind him and lashing him roughly to his mule, the outlaws led him south along the road he had just traveled. They rode for three days until they came to the outskirts of Brownsville. The outlaws and their prisoner skirted the town to the west and crossed the Rio Grande into Mexico.

The rancher was not to see Texas again for nearly four years. After traveling several miles into Mexico to the open range country near the city of Monterrey, the bandits joined up with several others of their kind. The rancher was forced to perform menial chores for the outlaws as they roamed the countryside stealing horses and cattle and robbing and killing travelers.

One morning, all the bandits rode away from the camp except for the prisoner and an old man who was in charge of the horses. A substantial herd of cattle had been spotted on a ranch a full day's ride to the west, and the outlaws believed the animals would bring a good price north of the border.

The old man, who was crippled and very hard of hearing, spent most of his time sleeping and ignored the prisoner for the entire morning. Following a late afternoon meal, the wrangler crawled into a low-ceilinged dirt house and immediately fell asleep.

When the prisoner was sure the old man was not watching, he stole a horse and rode away toward the Rio Grande as fast as he could. For several days he traveled, stopping only to take water for himself and his mount from a pond or spring. Tired, hungry, and weak from exposure, he eventually made his way back to his ranch near Brownsville.

After resting up from his ordeal, the rancher was ready to ride north toward Beeville and recover the $40,000 in gold he had cached nearly four years earlier.

The task was not to be as easy as he had thought it would. While he was gone, ranchers throughout South Texas had begun to use barbed wire and had fenced in large sections of their holdings. In some cases, the old Brownsville to Beeville road was diverted as a result of this practice. Much of the country was heavily stocked with cattle and the once lush rangelands looked overgrazed. Nothing about the land seemed familiar.

After crossing the Nueces River, the rancher tried several times to retrace his route to the two large oak trees, but the campsite where the $40,000 in gold had been buried was never found.

The Rock-Pen Treasure

Daniel Dunham was a bandit who buried what may have been one of the largest treasures in the state of Texas. It was a treasure that would have made him and his fellow desperadoes incredibly wealthy, but because of an unfortunate turn of events, neither he nor any of his comrades were able to return for it.

Dunham had been a petty criminal most of his life. As a child, he was abandoned and had to survive on the mean streets of coastal Texas towns by begging and stealing. Dunham fell in with outlaws, and for the rest of his life, he robbed and rustled, always hoping for a huge payday when he could finally retire from banditry and take life easy.

While holding up travelers in remote parts of South Texas, Dunham and his fellows learned of a rich gold mine near a small town in the Mexican state of Tamaulipas. Thinking this could be the payday of which they often dreamed, the outlaws crossed the border to raid the area.

Locating the mine and adjacent smelter with no difficulty, the outlaws confiscated enough bars of gold to fully load twenty-eight pack mules. Stopping briefly at the little town near the mine as they escaped to the north, the outlaws sacked the church and stole enough golden chalices, candle holders, and statuary to burden three more mules. With this incredible store of riches, the bandits herded the pack train northward as fast as they could travel, fearing pursuit from Mexican authorities.

On crossing the Rio Grande, the bandits did not linger. The border meant little to the residents on both sides, and forays and pursuits into both countries were common. Dunham insisted the men keep going north until they were safely within the confines of Austin and, pausing only long enough to feed and water themselves and their livestock, the outlaws undertook the journey of more than 250 miles.

Within sight of the Nueces River in what is now McMullen County, one of the bandits noticed a rising cloud of dust far to the rear of the column. Thinking it was from pursuing Mexican soldiers, Dunham ordered the outlaws to make a stand.

A level hill somewhat higher than the surrounding terrain looked defensible to Dunham. Arriving at the summit of the low hill, he noticed that due west was a shallow ravine. In the ravine, spring water trickled out from under a large rock.

As scouts watched the approaching dust trail, the remaining outlaws dug a large hole in the center of the flat-topped hill. When it was deep enough, the packs containing the gold bullion and church artifacts were lowered into it. Several men hastily scraped dirt and rock over the excavation while others constructed a crude breastwork of larger rocks which lay in profusion nearby. As the riders in the distance grew closer, the outlaws, along with most of their horses and mules, awaited them in the circular rock pen on top of the low hill. The horses and mules milling about inside the enclosure packed the loose earth so that it looked exactly like the rest of the area.

To the outlaws' surprise, the riders were not Mexican soldiers but rather a band of renegade Indians along with a few Mexican bandits.

They attacked. For several hours, a battle raged, and several members of both parties were killed. As sundown approached, only Dunham and one other outlaw remained alive in the fortress. Then Dunham's companion took a bullet in the eye. Dunham counted seven raiders still alive.

As darkness descended on the South Texas brush country, Dunham decided his best chance for survival lay in escape. He wormed his way through a break in the rock pen and crawled off. Morning found him several miles away to the north—tired, bleeding, and hungry, but alive. Several months later, Dunham arrived in Kansas City, where he chose to live out the remainder of his life.

Throughout the years following the attack on the pack train by the raiders on the obscure flat-topped hill in McMullen County, several hunters, prospectors, and ranchers chanced upon the rock pen, but none was ever aware of the great treasure that lay just two feet below the surface.

When, Dunham, old now, lay dying in a Kansas City hospital, he had a will prepared, and his meager possessions were designated for his wife and children. When the will was completed, Dunham asked the attorney to write down the story of the rock-pen treasure. Dunham dictated it to him, providing precise directions and including landmarks like the ravine and the spring.

Over the years, the manuscript containing Dunham's version of how the huge treasure came to be cached in McMullen County passed through several hands and eventually wound up in the possession of a rancher named Matt Kivlin, a resident of Live Oak County. Kivlin showed the manuscript to members of his family and forbade his own sons to engage in any search for the treasure. Though it has never been proven, many believed Kivlin was related to the outlaw Dunham and, for reasons that remain mysterious to this day, never attempted to recover what must be the equivalent of several million dollars worth of gold.

In 1866, a rancher named Pete McNeill was riding in a wagon with his wife, traveling from the town of Tilden southward toward the settlement of Lagarto. McNeill had a saddled horse tied behind the wagon. As they crossed land owned by a neighboring rancher named Shiner, McNeill spotted an unmarked calf several yards off the road. In those days, an unbranded calf, or maverick, was considered unowned and belonged to the first person to brand it.

Seizing his branding iron from the bed of the wagon, McNeill leaped on his horse and chased and captured the maverick. After tying down the animal, the rancher looked around for some wood with which to build a fire and heat the iron. As he gathered a few limbs of dry wood, he noticed he was inside some kind of old, tumbled-down rock pen on top of a flat hill. Assuming it was what was left of the primitive corral of some rancher who had long ago moved away, McNeill thought nothing of it. He branded the calf, and after drinking from a small spring he found in a nearby ravine, he and his wife went on to Lagarto.

Several years later, Matt Kivlin passed away and members of his family freely related the story of the rock-pen treasure cache. When McNeill heard the tale, he was certain that the old rock pen where he branded the maverick years earlier was the site of the buried fortune.

McNeill tried several times to find the flat-topped hill, but he claimed the country had changed so much he could never get his bearings.

Not long afterward, a deer hunter used the rock pen as a temporary camp, completely unaware of its relationship to the buried treasure. The location, with the protecting walls of the pen and the cool, clear water of the nearby spring, was ideal. When told the story of Dunham's adventures, the deer hunter, like McNeill, tried several times to find the hill again but never could.

In the years since the rock pen was thrown together in that isolated location in McMullen County, the original structure has no doubt fallen into ruin and disrepair, with walls collapsed and rocks scattered about the hilltop.

Away from any major road or trail, the flat-topped hill—remote and desolate—is likely to elude hunters for the rock-pen treasure for many years to come.

South Texas Silver

In the early 1870s, John Fogg owned a prosperous livery stable in downtown Corpus Christi. The bustling town was an important destination and stopover for seagoing as well as overland travelers on their way to settle newly opened lands to the west, and the demand for riding stock was great. As the population grew, Fogg hired two men to assist him in running the business, and all three often worked around the clock in order to accommodate the increase of customers.

One afternoon as Fogg was shoveling out some grain for his stable mounts, a very old and bent Mexican walked in out of the hot sun and stood in the shade just inside the large door. When Fogg asked if he could help, the old fellow, in halting English, said he had been traveling for a long time and had not eaten for several days. He told Fogg he would work in his stables all day for a simple meal of beans and tortillas.

Fogg could tell the man had seen hardship in his life—his bent back suggested many years of labor in the fields, and the scarred and withered hands and face bespoke a lifetime in the out-of-doors. Realizing the old man was near the point of starvation, Fogg invited him home and fed him.

That evening, Fogg told the old man he was welcome to sleep in the livery stable and in the morning could begin work cleaning the pens. The old Mexican thanked Fogg and retired for the night.

For a full week, the Mexican labored at the stables. Fogg claimed that despite his great age, he was the best worker he had ever employed. Fogg was about to offer him a permanent job when the old man came to the livery stable owner one morning and said it was time for him to leave.

Fogg asked where he was headed. Sitting on the long, low bench by the wide doorway of the frame building, the Mexican told Fogg a fascinating tale of hidden treasure located about a three-day ride to the northwest.

As a youth, the Mexican had been conscripted by the Mexican Army to help tend the horses and mules of a large pack train that was transporting silver bullion from the rich mines at San Saba to the church repositories in Mexico City. The small company of soldiers, led by a young captain on his first assignment, left the mines early one morning with twenty-one burro-loads of silver bars, all packed tightly in leather sacks tied to the backs of the animals.

In the rugged brush country in southwestern McMullen County, the party was set upon by Indians, and the captain ordered the men and mules into a nearby ravine between two low, flat-topped hills. Once in the rocky gap, the young officer had the mules unpacked and the silver stashed in several large cracks and joints found in the weathered limestone. While some of the men concealed the caches by stacking rocks against them, others prepared to defend the position.

As the soldiers readied their weapons, the captain sent the young Mexican to get water from a spring in an adjoining ravine. The youngster, eager to help, ran to the spring. As he was filling vessels, he heard the sudden loud drum of hoofbeats and turned to see several dozen Indians racing down the adjacent ravine toward the soldiers. Cut off from the troops, the boy concealed himself in the reeds by the spring.

The Indians won the fierce two-hour battle. For a long time, the youth could barely discern the sounds of the

Indians as they plundered items of equipment they wished to keep. The sounds continued well past sundown, and then silence descended on the area. The boy remained hidden in the reeds until sunrise of the next day. He cautiously returned to the neighboring ravine and the scene of struggle. The sights there sent chills of horror through the youth, and it was all he could do to maintain control and not go mad. About him lay the carnage of battle: the bloody forms of men, horses, and mules. All the soldiers had been scalped and horribly mutilated and their bodies stripped of clothing and weapons. Saddles and other gear had been taken, but the boy finally found some food the raiders had overlooked. As he prepared a hasty meal, he noticed the caches of silver bars had not disturbed. Shaken, he managed to choke down some food before he struck out south toward Mexico City.

His trip was long and arduous. He often went days without food, and water was scarce in the arid brush country. His boots soon wore out, and his feet were torn and blistered before they toughened.

Occasionally the boy would encounter raiding parties of Indians and be forced to hide until the danger passed. Once he cowered in a shallow cave for three days and nights while Indians camped within a few yards of his position.

Months passed, and the youth finally arrived in Mexico City, where he related the events of the massacre. The Mexican authorities charged the boy with desertion and sentenced him to prison, where he languished for thirty-seven years.

When he was finally released, the Mexican, now fifty years of age, went to work as a field hand on the farms near Cuernavaca. As he toiled, he often dreamed of returning to the Texas brush country and retrieving the vast treasure hoard he felt certain was still hidden in the rocks of the shallow ravine.

Many more years passed, and the Mexican, now an old man, decided to undertake the long journey to Texas. After months of traveling on foot, he finally arrived in Corpus Christi, where he met John Fogg.

After hearing the old man's story, Fogg got excited at the prospect of recovering the silver and asked to join the Mexican in pursuit of the treasure. With the old man's consent, Fogg hired three men to accompany them. He made arrangements for his two employees to operate his livery stable for a few weeks, and within days, he led the search party toward the hilly, rocky country where the Nueces River makes a turn and flows toward the northeast.

On the evening of the third day, the party set up camp on the rocky flats not far from the river. With difficulty, the Mexican climbed to the top of a nearby hill and scanned the countryside. When he returned, he told Fogg and the others that he recognized the country and knew exactly which direction to travel in the morning to find the ravine that contained the caches of Mexican silver.

As Fogg and the Mexican discussed what they would each do with their share of the treasure, one of the men cooked venison from a freshly-killed deer for supper. When the meat was ready, Fogg pulled a bottle of whiskey from a saddlebag and called for a celebration on this eve of their impending discovery. The men ate well and drank a large quantity of the fiery alcohol, finally retiring to their blankets well after midnight.

Just before dawn, Fogg awoke to the groans of the old Mexican. The livery stable operator could see the old man was in severe pain, clutching at his stomach and muttering prayers to his saints. Apparently he had eaten too much venison and drunk far too much whiskey and was now suffering for it. His cries awakened the others, and soon everyone in camp was trying to soothe the ailing Mexican. By the time the sun was up an hour, the old man was dead.

Fogg, frustrated at coming so close to the treasure and then losing his only link to it, was at a loss as to what to do next. He climbed to the same low hill the Mexican ascended the previous evening and tried to discern what he had seen, searching hopefully for some clue to the mysterious ravine. For several days, Fogg and his companions explored ravines for miles around, but they found nothing.

Discouraged and dejected, the party finally returned to Corpus Christi, and the treasure of silver bullion hurriedly stashed many years ago remains hidden in a secluded ravine in southeastern McMullen County.

The Bottomless-Pit Treasure

Northeast of the Rio Grande in Dimmit County, there may still exist a large, oval spring of clear water historically known as the Grand Rock Water Hole. The spring was for many years a favored location of travelers through this remote region of South Texas, and the flat ground around the water hole bore evidence of many camps, Indian, Mexican, and Anglo.

A fascinating legend is associated with this spring, a legend concerning several million dollars worth of gold and silver which was allegedly hidden in the depths of Grand Rock Water Hole, a treasure awaiting recovery by anyone who can find the spring and locate the fabulous hoard in it. The legend also claims the spring is bottomless.

In the first decade of the nineteenth century, Texas was still part of Mexico, and San Antonio was the commercial center for this northern realm. Many wealthy Spaniards and Mexicans made San Antonio their home, and trade and travel between this burgeoning community and the capital of Mexico City far to the south was lively.

As commerce picked up and businesses and banks became established in San Antonio, pack trains carrying goods and money between San Antonio and Mexico City were frequent. Gold and silver coins and bullion were regularly shipped from one city to the other.

Sometime in the early summer of 1803, a pack train consisting of thirty mules loaded with millions of dollars' worth of gold and silver coins as well as many bars of each mineral left Mexico City early one spring morning bound for San Antonio. Several drivers were hired to lead the mules on the long journey north, and the pack train was accompanied by fifty well-armed Mexican soldiers intent on keeping the treasure safe from bandits and Indians that might be encountered along the way.

The party was led by one Captain Palacio Flores. Flores was a favorite of General Santa Anna and came from a prominent Mexican family. A bright future was predicted for the young captain, and if he performed well on this assignment, he would be considered for a promotion and a transfer to a position of authority in the capitol.

The journey north was uneventful. Passing through the beautiful mountains and plains of eastern Mexico, the party paused to rest at cities such as San Luis Potosí and Monterrey. They encountered neither Indians nor bandits along the way, and the pack train made excellent progress.

Their route crossed the Rio Grande about fifty miles upstream from Laredo and took the party into the rugged, rocky, brush-covered hills of South Texas. Almost immediately, the guards saw men on horseback watching the pack train from safe distances. Before leaving Mexico City, Flores had been warned by other soldiers who had previously traveled this road of the ruthlessness of the bandits on it.

Nervously, the soldiers kept scanning the horizons and ravines for any sign of attack by the outlaws. The watchers were often spotted, but no attack came. It was clear, however, that the pack train was being followed.

On the first evening after crossing the Rio Grande, Flores selected a campsite and ordered the mules unloaded and the packs of gold and silver stacked in the center. Guards were doubled, and the soldiers and drivers spent an uneasy and restless night anticipating an attack from the bandits. The night went by quietly, however, and when morning came, the treasure was loaded onto the mules and the pack train wound its way along the tortuous trail toward San Antonio, some 120 miles northeast. Because of the rocky and broken ground, travel was slow, and Flores, often referring to a map, made plans to camp at a location known as Grand Rock Water Hole.

On this leg of the trip, Flores noticed that the number of men observing their progress from the nearby hills had increased to nearly thirty and that they were venturing closer and closer to the pack train.

Flores soon arrived at Pena Creek and followed it for several miles. Late on the afternoon of the second day after crossing the Rio Grande, the party rounded a sharp bend in the creek and several dozen yards beyond came upon the well-known spring. Captain Flores again ordered the treasure unloaded from the mules and had the drivers stack it in a central location near the water hole.

Flores decided they would stay here for two or three days while they and the animals rested up for the final portion of the trip into San Antonio.

Following the evening meal, Flores again doubled the sentries, and the camp spent another fearful night, constantly alert to the possibility of an attack from the mysterious riders. All was quiet that night, and throughout the entire next day, none of the riders were seen.

Flores, believing the threat of attack had disappeared, decided not to post extra guards the second night. The young, inexperienced captain was beginning to believe he and his soldiers were overreacting to the presence of the riders, and perhaps overrating the threat from bandits. The captain, like many of his kind, was convinced his soldiers had firepower and bravery sufficient to repel any kind of attack. That evening, the soldiers and drivers slept with only a handful of sentries standing guard.

As the men made breakfast the next morning, dozens of armed riders thundered up out of adjacent ravines and the camp. Several soldiers were killed in the first rush.

The bandits wheeled and regrouped to surge once again into the stricken throng of Mexicans, and Flores organized a contingent of musketeers into a skirmish line to fend off the invaders. The soldiers readied their weapons and strapped on their swords, and Flores ordered the drivers to throw the packs of gold and silver coins and bullion into the spring. To lose the wealth he had been entrusted with to bandits would be to disgrace himself and jeopardize his career as a soldier, and Flores intended to do all he could to keep the outlaws from taking the treasures. When the battle was over, he would recover the gold and silver from the spring and deliver it to San Antonio.

The second rush from the bandits resulted in the loss of several more Mexican soldiers. For the first time, Flores began to fear the outcome of the battle. When the last of the packs was tossed into the clear waters of the spring, Flores himself yanked his saber from its scabbard and went to the front line to join his men in repelling the invaders.

On the third and final charge into the unprepared swarm of soldiers, the bandits clearly dominated. Flores was killed, and soon troopers and drivers were running in all directions seeking shelter in the ravines. The bandits, their lust for killing sharpened by their victory, chased down the panicked men, killing many of them.

One of the drivers, an elderly man named Alejandro Lajero, took refuge in a clump of trees and escaped notice of the raging bandits. While the raiders fought over the choice mounts and the spoils of the camp, Lajero cowered in his hiding place until dark. When he believed it was safe to do so, the old man crept silently away and continued the journey to San Antonio on foot.

Several days later, Lajero, weak and near starvation, arrived in the city and related the incident of the massacre at the Grand Rock Water Hole. Several men in authority reluctantly suggested assembling a mounted force and returning to the area to punish the bandits and recover the treasure, but it was clear they feared the outlaw element in that part of Texas. They decided to wait.

As time passed, what little enthusiasm there was for returning to Grand Rock Water Hole diminished. Soon the hidden Mexican treasure in the depths of the spring faded from the thoughts of San Antonio's citizens, and the incident was gradually forgotten.

Many years went by, and the treasure in the spring came to mind again in 1893 when a reporter for a San Antonio newspaper found several references to the event in some obscure archival material he ran across. The reporter tracked down information about to whom the gold and silver was to be delivered some ninety years earlier and contacted the descendants. Soon, the heirs organized a group to try to find and recover the fortune.

With considerable difficulty, the search party finally found the Grand Rock Water Hole. The area around the spring was littered with the bleached bones of men and animals. True to the descriptions they had, the waters of the spring were clear, cool, and delicious. Try as they might, though, they could not plumb the bottom of the pool.

The searchers used long poles to probe, but were still unable make contact. Two members of the party tried to swim to the bottom, but they finally climbed out and said the waters went beyond the depths a man could go.

Tying ropes together and weighting one end with a large rock, they lowered a line several hundred feet long into the spring and never touched bottom. The search party gave up and returned to San Antonio. There is no record of any further effort to recover the treasure.

According to researchers who have investigated the accounts of the Grand Rock Water Hole treasure, the spring was on the banks near Pena Creek in Dimmit County, a few miles northwest of the town of Carrizo Springs. Some area residents have claimed the spring ran dry. Others say it silted in years ago from the creek's flooding. Still others claim the spring is just as it was when Captain Flores and his soldiers were there, and that somewhere deep below the cool blue waters lies a great fortune in gold and silver.

Chest of Silver Coins

Many lost and buried treasures about which tales are told are never found. Once in a while, though, a lost hoard *is* discovered, sometimes accidentally, sometimes as a result of great effort and planning. This story concerns a chest of silver coins buried by a miserly South Texas cattle rancher and found many years later by pure luck.

Old man Tolbert ran a prosperous ranch along the Frio River in what is now Frio County. Neighboring ranchers admired Tolbert's livestock and marveled at the old man's ability to keep them well-watered, well-fed, and healthy in this sparse and arid county, but Tolbert himself always acted as if he were on the verge of bankruptcy and poverty.

Tolbert never married, hired few hands to work on his ranch, and lived in a ramshackle cabin. On the few occasions he went into town for supplies, the parsimonious rancher seldom bought more than the barely essential foodstuffs required to keep a person alive. His ranch hands often had to supplement their meager meals by shooting and cooking wild rabbits and harvesting cactus fruit. The ranch hands, it was said, often went without pay.

For all his stinginess, Tolbert was a shrewd trader and businessman, and major transactions often left him with satchels of money. His cattle deals often involved hundreds of head at a time, and one of his biggest and most consistent customers was the U.S. Army.

Tolbert always insisted that payment for his cattle be in silver coins, a policy from which he never deviated. He also distrusted banks, and as soon as a sale was done, he would return to his ranch immediately and hide his coins. Over the years, it has been estimated that Tolbert amassed a large fortune in silver, a fortune that was buried in several locations on his property.

When the old man finally died, leaving neither a will nor heirs, many residents of this part of South Texas presumed his extensive wealth was still hidden someplace on his ranch. The old ranch house was practically torn apart by treasure hunters, and dozens of holes were dug in and around the yard as people searched for the silver.

Several years after Tolbert passed away, a man named Berry purchased his ranch and moved onto the property. Berry, like his predecessor, built up a fine herd of cattle and became a successful rancher in the community. Berry was aware of the stories of Tolbert's buried treasure supposedly located someplace on the ranch, but he was far too busy running a good ranch to try to chase it down.

Berry hired several ranch hands to help him with his cattle operations. One of them, an elderly Mexican too infirm to ride, was assigned chores around the ranch house, barn, and yard. One morning, Berry and the Mexican took down Tolbert's old corral fence with the intention of enlarging the structure and replacing the old rotted posts. The two men made short work of it and stacked the old fence-posts by the ranch house for firewood.

After marking the outline of the new corral, Berry had the old Mexican dig a new set of postholes. Berry went to sit and relax in the shade of his newly constructed ranch house as other ranch hands dragged in freshly cut posts from the surrounding hills.

Berry whittled as he watched the old man work on the second hole. It was clear the Mexican was tired from the morning's labors and withering in the heat of the South Texas day. The rancher decided he would take a turn at digging the postholes himself in a little while.

As he worked on the third hole, the Mexican's spade struck something hard just below the topsoil. The sound was almost metallic, and Berry momentarily stopped his whittling to look. The Mexican jammed the spade into the ground again, and again it was blocked. The Mexican looked over at Berry and indicated he was going to rest for awhile. Berry waved him on, rose from his bench, and walked over to the corral to pick up the digging chore.

Having often dug postholes in South Texas soil, Berry had sometimes had to use an iron bar to break up the hard dirt. He selected an iron rod of suitable length from a pile of tools near the tack shed and set to work on the hole the old Mexican had begun.

As he plunged the bar into the ground, Berry realized that something metal lay just beneath the thin layer of loose dirt. Scraping away rock, soil, and debris with his hands, Berry soon saw the top of a large metal chest. Using the iron bar and the shovel, the rancher removed several bucket-loads of dirt from above and around the buried object.

The chest was bulky and heavy. Berry couldn't lift it from the hole. He tied two ropes around it and pulled it out with a draft horse.

In the shade of the ranch house, Berry pried the lid off the metal chest and was stunned to see its contents: the chest was almost completely filled with silver coins. Berry presumed it to be a portion of Tolbert's wealth.

Far into the evening, Berry counted the money contained in the chest. How much it amounted to was never revealed, but the next morning, Berry loaded the chest onto a wagon, drove into the nearby town of Pearsall, and made the largest deposit in the small town bank's history.

Berry was now a very wealthy man, and though his cattle ranch prospered over the years, he eventually turned its operation over to others. A few years after finding Tolbert's treasure chest, Berry moved to San Antonio and retired to a life of luxury.

There are some who claim Berry did not recover all of Tolbert's fortune.

Several years after Berry left, two travelers arrived in the area on a rickety buckboard asking directions to the Tolbert Ranch. Following what appeared to be an old map, the two were seen driving their old wagon down a seldom-used trail leading into a ravine about a half mile from Tolbert's old ranch house site. Here the two men apparently set up camp, far from the view of anyone passing by.

Early the next morning, the men were seen leaving the ravine. As one drove the team that pulled the wagon, the other held a shotgun across his lap and looked around as if guarding the wagon against attack. On their way out of the area, they refused to converse with anyone. They disappeared down the road leading to Corpus Christi, never to be seen again.

A neighboring rancher who had seen the pair the previous afternoon decided to investigate their campsite. On his way into the ravine, the rancher noticed that the outgoing wheel ruts made by the wagon were much deeper than those entering. Leaving, the wagon was obviously transporting a heavy load.

At the strangers' campsite near the bottom of the ravine, the rancher found a freshly dug excavation beneath a large live oak tree. The rancher could clearly see the imprint in the moist earth of what must have been a large chest. Nearby he found a broken hasp and a pair of twisted hinges.

When the rancher told his story around town the next day, the consensus was that the two strangers somehow knew about another of Tolbert's treasure caches and, with the help of a map, were able to locate it.

Many believe there are more chests filled with silver coins buried on the old Tolbert Ranch. Even today when one visits the site of the old ranch house, it is not uncommon to find freshly dug holes in the yard—evidence that the search continues.

The Gulf Coast

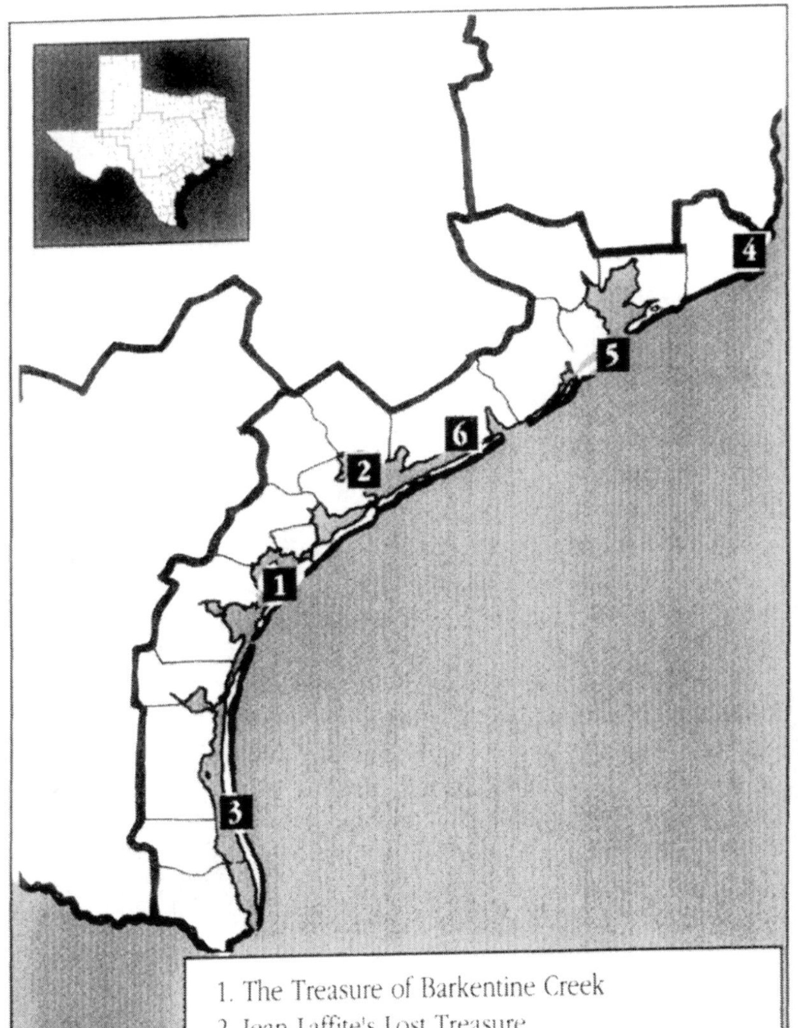

1. The Treasure of Barkentine Creek
2. Jean Laffite's Lost Treasure
3. John Singer's Padre Island Treasure
4. The Curse of the Neches River Treasure
5. The Shipwrecks on Deer Island
6. The Treasure of Matagorda Bay

The Treasure of Barkentine Creek

During September, 1822, a series of hurricanes and tropical storms developed in the Atlantic, ripped across the Gulf of Mexico, and slammed onto the Texas coast between Corpus Christi and Galveston, dropping several inches of rainfall for hundreds of miles inland. Many seagoing vessels remained tied up in coastal ports for weeks at a time waiting for a break in the storms.

Early in the first week of September, a Spanish barkentine carrying hundreds of gold ingots and several wooden casks filled with gold coins sailed from the port at Veracruz, Mexico, toward a rendezvous with several other Spanish vessels waiting in Galveston harbor. The ships, all flying the Spanish flag and carrying great quantities of treasure, were to assemble and undertake together the long journey across the Atlantic to Spain to deliver their rich cargoes to the Spanish crown.

When the barkentine left Veracruz, the weather was relatively calm. As she sailed north toward the Texas coast, however, the skies grew dark and the seas choppy. By the time the boat approached Corpus Christi, it was clear that a major storm was advancing on the Texas coast. The captain of the Spanish ship, Diego Soto, believed that if he kept to the relatively calm waters of the narrow channel between the Texas coastline and the nearly one-hundred-mile-long Matagorda Island, he would be able to cheat the storm and get to the port of Galveston on schedule and without damage.

The buffering effect Soto thought the narrow island would have against the storm was almost nonexistent as the hurricane surged northwestward onto the coastal flats. Fearing the high winds and violent waves would capsize his ship, the captain steered into the wide mouth of a river in search of shallow water. The river, which many researchers believe to have been the Mission River, was swollen far above flood stage from rain and runoff and provided ample draft for the Spanish barkentine.

The terrific wind blew the ship several miles up the flooded river and into a tributary where it eventually ran aground. When the storm abated almost two days later and the level of the creek dropped, the ship was securely mired in the soft mud. Only another great flood could possibly lift and release her.

Several crew members perished in the storm, having been thrown overboard in the raging sea. About a dozen survivors, including Captain Soto, abandoned the hopelessly stranded ship and its contents and undertook to walk to the coast in hope of rescue. During the trek, the small party of hungry and unarmed sailors was attacked by a roving band of Karankawa Indians and all were killed.

Years passed, and the stranded barkentine with its load of treasure reposed on the coastal prairie by the creek up which it had traveled. Spanish officials presumed the vessel sank during the storm somewhere in the Gulf, and they never initiated a search for it.

Sometime in the 1840s, a raiding party of Comanche Indians, traveling far south of their normal range, entered Karankawa country to raid Indian villages along the coast, stealing horses and taking captives to be used as slaves.

The Comanches encountered the long-forgotten ship while riding across the coastal prairie in what is now

Refugio County. Having never seen such a structure before, the Indians cautiously entered the rotting ship and explored it. Nothing inside the vessel held much interest for the Comanches save for the several casks of gold coins. The Comanches had little use for money, but they knew from experience that the coins were eagerly accepted by white traders as payment for guns and provisions, and in the hands of the tribe's craftsmen, the gold could be turned into fine jewelry and ornaments.

After loading eight gold-filled casks onto several stolen ponies, the Comanches were about to leave for their plains homelands far to the northwest when they were attacked by a mounted band of Karankawas intent on regaining their horses and exacting vengeance on their enemies.

The Comanches fled from the ship with the Karankawas close behind. The two groups rode and fought for nearly two miles across the coastal prairie until the Comanches decided to make a stand. At the top of a low grassy knoll, they dismounted, killed several horses, and arranged them in a crude semi-circular breastwork behind which they crouched and fired arrows into the pursuing Karankawas.

In the middle of this protective ring, two of the Comanches scraped out a hole and buried the casks of gold coins. The fighting lasted for approximately an hour, and the Karankawas were eventually dispersed. Most of the horses taken by the Comanches escaped, however, and the casks of coins remained buried atop the knoll when the Indians finally departed. The knoll is believed to be northwest of the town of Refugio.

In 1855, an elderly Comanche who had participated in the battle with the Karankawas returned to the area with his wife and children in an attempt to retrieve the gold. They camped on the prairie for several days but were unsuccessful in locating the grassy knoll where he and his fellow warriors had fought.

The Comanche and his family traveled toward the coast and eventually found the old barkentine. The weathered ship had sunk deeper, and the interior was almost entirely filled with sand, mud, and debris. Unknown to the Comanche, hundreds of gold ingots lay just a few feet under the cover of dirt. The Indian searched the wreck once again for casks of gold coins but found none.

After the Civil War, white settlers from the southern states, attracted by the abundance of land, began to move onto the rich coastal grasslands in large numbers. The prairie around Refugio County held considerable promise, and a man named Fagan established a ranch of several thousand acres.

Neighbors told Fagan of the Spanish barkentine somewhere on his ranch, and as he badly needed timbers with which to construct a house, he searched for and found the long-abandoned vessel. Unaware that there was a great fortune in gold ingots somewhere in the ship's mud-filled interior, Fagan systematically disassembled the craft and took away the timbers to use in building his house.

Having taken what wood was salvageable, Fagan left the rest to rot in the hot and humid coastal climate, and after another three decades, little evidence remained of the beached craft. The small tributary up which the Spanish ship had been blown during the storm of nearly a hundred years earlier was called Barkentine Creek by local people, but few know its exact location today.

Somewhere close to this creek under a thin cover of sand, soil, and prairie grasses lies a king's ransom in gold ingots, likely worth several million dollars at today's values.

Jean Laffite's Lost Booty

Of all the pirates that sailed the Gulf of Mexico, none was more noteworthy or notorious than Jean Laffite, a dashing and colorful pirate who has been the focus of many tales of lost and buried treasure. Much of what has been told about this buccaneer over the past century-and-a-half has been consigned to the category of legend, but many of his exploits and much of his wealth have been documented. The likelihood that Laffite left behind rich treasures of hidden gold, silver, and jewels is great.

Jean Laffite moved his base of operations from the Louisiana coast to Galveston Island in 1819 after being driven from the former by the United States Navy. On arriving at Galveston Island, Laffite encountered a rival band of pirates that had taken up residence several months earlier. With no hesitation, Laffite attacked the sanctuary, drove the other freebooters from the area, and established a headquarters in an abandoned Spanish fortress which stood about a half mile west of what is now the Galveston Yacht Basin. From here, Laffite carried out many successful raids on Spanish treasure ships carrying gold and silver from the Americas to the European homeland.

Laffite prospered at this enterprise, but he could not resist attacking American ships from time to time. The continued assaults on U.S. vessels came to the attention of government officials who in turn ordered the *U.S.S. Interprise,* captained by a dedicated officer named Kearney, to Galveston Island to rid the region of Jean Laffite and his pirates. After several days of discussions and negotiations between Laffite and Kearney, the pirate chieftain hanged two of his men he claimed were responsible for the attacks on American ships, hoping the gesture would appease Kearney. Not to be pacified so easily, Kearney ordered the guns of the *Interprise* aimed toward the island and gave Laffite thirty days to vacate.

Four days before the period was to expire, Laffite's favorite ship, the *Pride,* ran aground near the mouth of the Lavaca River, fractured some planks, and sank. The *Pride* was known to have been carrying a great quantity of treasure taken during raids of several Spanish vessels.

With the *Interprise* patrolling the waters nearby, Laffite quickly divided some of the treasure among his men, and with the help of two trusted friends, a great chest filled with gold coins and jewelry along with two canvas sacks filled with silver bars were carried to shore for burial.

Laffite and his men hauled the treasure several hundred yards across the salt marsh, chose a place, and buried it.

Laffite took a compass reading and a bearing on two nearby mottes, or groves of trees—Kentucky Motte and Mauldin Motte. The pirate made some notes in his journal, and when he finished, he took a long brass rod he had carried from the ship and shoved it deep into the ground just above the treasure until only about eight inches remained visible.

A few days later, Laffite was driven from the island and, according to legend, never returned to recover the fortune in gold, silver, and jewels hidden in the salt marsh. Laffite reportedly told his two trusted helpers that he was going to a secret location north of the Red River, and he instructed them to return to New Orleans and live honest lives. He also told them that if they returned to the site of the buried treasure at the end of three years and found it still there, they could have it.

One of the men died within a few months from malaria, but not before relating the story of the buried treasure to a friend. Using the directions provided by the former pirate, the friend made several unsuccessful attempts to locate the chest and silver bars. The other pirate who helped Laffite bury the treasure never returned to the site, choosing instead to remain in New Orleans and raise a family. As an old man, the former buccaneer told the story of the buried chest of gold and jewels to his two sons. With great enthusiasm and apparently certain of their ability to find the treasure, the sons organized an expedition to the Lavaca River marsh, but they too failed.

Several years passed, and a rancher named Hill settled on the land at the junction of the Lavaca River and Galveston Bay and stocked the grassy marshes with fine horses and cattle. Hill hired a black man to tend his livestock and entrusted the fellow to run horses and cattle out onto the marsh during the day to graze and return them to the farmyard in the evening to be penned up.

While watching the livestock during the day, the hired hand would sometimes nap on the grassy sward. One warm afternoon as he tended the stock on horseback, he grew drowsy and searched for a good place to stretch out on the soft ground. Dismounting, he looked around for something to which he could tie his horse and found the tip of a brass rod poking out of the soil nearby. After hitching the horse to the rod, the man reclined a few paces away and dozed off.

The horse, unaccustomed to being staked, nearly pulled the rod out of the soft ground. When the hired hand awoke from his nap, he completely withdrew the rod and carried it with him when he returned the stock to the ranch headquarters, intending to show it to his employer.

Hill was familiar with the tale of Laffite's buried treasure, and when he saw the long brass rod, he knew it immediately for what it was. The hired hand told Hill about tying his mount to the rod and the rancher asked to be taken there early the next morning. Though they searched all day, the two men were unable to find the spot from which the rod had been pulled.

In 1870, a man went turkey hunting near the mouth of the Lavaca River. Spotting a flock of birds several dozen yards away, the hunter got down on his hands and knees and crawled through the cover of thick grass toward his quarry. As he was creeping along on all fours, his knee struck hard against something partially buried in the ground, and when he turned to inspect the source of his pain, he found what looked like a small pile of bricks. Curious about why bricks would be in this remote section of the marsh, the turkey hunter put one in his shot pouch, intending to examine it later.

At home that evening, the hunter removed the heavy brick from the pouch and showed it to his brother. The brother made some scratches on it and discovered the "brick" was pure silver! Not unfamiliar with the story of Jean Laffite's buried treasure, the two men deduced the long-lost pirate cache had finally been discovered.

When the brothers returned to the approximate location the next day, however, they couldn't find the remaining bricks. The two men searched several miles of the grassy marsh, but the region was so similar throughout that it was difficult to pinpoint any specific location. Prominent in the distance as they searched were Kentucky Motte and Mauldin Motte, but neither of the men were aware of their relationship to the cache they were looking for.

One man may have actually found Laffite's buried treasure chest, but it is likely he removed only a few gold coins. An eccentric old fellow known locally as Crazy Ben was a frequent visitor to the waterfront bars of Galveston during the 1880s. Crazy Ben was well known to most of the residents, but he was seldom friendly with anyone. The old man was never known to work, and he lived in squalor in an old shack near the mouth of the Lavaca River. What distinguished Crazy Ben from the other patrons of the local alehouses was the fact that he paid for his drinks with gold Spanish coins.

Crazy Ben often related the story that he was once a cabin boy to Jean Laffite and that he secretly followed the notorious pirate leader across the salt marsh and watched him bury the treasure chest and bars of silver.

When the pirates fled the area several days later, Ben, no more than ten years old at the time, stayed on the south bank of Clear Creek near Galveston Bay, working as a fisherman and handyman, and occasionally begging for handouts.

Several years later, when Ben was certain Laffite was never going to return for the buried treasure, he went to the site, unearthed the chest, seized a handful of coins, and reburied the remainder. With the few coins in his possession, Ben was able to live well and drink his fill for several weeks. When he ran out of money, he returned to the chest for more.

Clearly an unambitious man, Crazy Ben preferred to drift around the bay area to the various taverns, spending his coins on ale. Occasionally, during alcohol-fogged conversations with fellow drinkers, Crazy Ben admitted to deriving his fortune from the buried treasure chest of the pirate Jean Laffite. Word of the old man's wealth spread throughout the area, and from time to time, someone would try to follow him out into the marsh. Ben was clever and always managed to elude them.

One evening after a full day of drinking at a local tavern, Crazy Ben staggered out of the establishment and down the street toward his shack. Almost immediately, two shadowy figures rose from behind a table and followed him into the night. It was the last time anyone saw Crazy Ben alive.

The next morning, Crazy Ben was found washed up on the shore of the bay near Clear Creek not far from his home. His throat had been slashed, and it is believed that he was killed because he refused to reveal the location of the Laffite treasure.

Many attempts to locate Jean Laffite's buried treasure chest have been made during the past 150 years. In the 1920s, a man arrived from Oklahoma with what he claimed were the original hand-written notes from Laffite's journal describing the location of the treasure chest. Although the man had no trouble locating the two prominent mottes, he was unable find the treasure.

Treasure hunters have resorted to high tech equipment, low-flying aircraft, and dowsing, but all efforts to find the hidden treasure have failed.

The search continues.

John Singer's Padre Island Treasure

In the middle of the nineteenth century, the brothers John and Isaac Merritt Singer were gaining fame as resourceful and enterprising inventors and businessmen. Of the two, Isaac was the best known, and had amassed a fortune as the president of the highly successful Singer Sewing Machine Company. John, the younger brother, was less concerned about wealth and success and resented the confines of the corporate bureaucracy. Rather than join his brother managing the family businesses, John preferred instead the many adventures life had to offer in Texas.

Though a devoted family man, John Singer indulged his passion to explore and experience new lands and new places. Singer took his wife and four sons with him on most of his travels, and it was during one of these family expeditions on the Gulf of Mexico that dramatic events occurred that were to forever alter the course of Singer's life.

The year was 1847, and John Singer, his wife, and children, accompanied by a hired deckhand, were exploring the Texas Gulf Coast in a three-masted schooner, stopping to camp on the many deserted islands and shores. It was a wonderful time for the Singer family, a time that would remain solidly in their memories for as long as they lived. As the Singers reveled in their paradisiacal life, they had no inkling that they were about to stumble onto several large buried treasure caches.

Early one morning, Singer steered his schooner, the *Alice Sadell,* from the harbor at Port Isabel near the Mexican border and sailed northward. Within an hour, the sky turned dark and the winds picked up. The Gulf's waves grew in height and intensity, pitching and rolling the ship. Singer, a relatively inexperienced seaman, believed the storm would soon pass and he chose to sail on, but within the hour it was clear to the adventurer that they were in the path of a hurricane.

As the storm's fury increased, Singer began to fear for the safety of his family. Torrents of rain fell upon the craft and visibility was nil. Lashed to the wheel, Singer had decided to seek a landing as soon as possible when the ship was caught in a fierce gust and hurled violently onto a sand beach. Though the ship was badly damaged, the passengers suffered no injuries and decided to wait out the storm by remaining inside the cabin of the ruined craft.

By morning, the storm had abated. Singer and the deckhand walked about the beach and correctly deduced they had landed on Padre Island, a sandy strip of land extending over a hundred miles from the Mexican border to Corpus Christi.

Singer's ship was not the first to be forced onto the island during a severe storm. Dozens of Spanish vessels transporting gold and silver from the rich mines in Mexico, Texas, and New Mexico, were often caught in hurricanes and either sunk off-shore or wrecked on the narrow, unpopulated island. In addition, bands of pirates frequented the area, using the island as a sometime headquarters and often burying their booty in the sands.

The Singer family went about the business of survival. While the deckhand rigged some of the ship's timbers and sails into a makeshift craft, John Singer, along with his wife and children, fashioned a tent from salvaged canvas.

The deckhand returned to Corpus Christi on the crude raft the next day to arrange for a rescue. The Singers contented themselves with exploring the portion of the island on which they were marooned. Mrs. Singer, undisturbed by the shipwreck, was actually happy to be on the island. She never cared for traveling on the seas and was relieved to be on solid ground. The children, sharing their father's lust for adventure, ran up and down the beach collecting shells and crabs.

After a few days, the Singers saw their accidental island home as a kind of paradise and decided to stay. When the rescue ship finally arrived, Singer told the captain their intention to settle on the island and sent him away.

The Singers were able to catch fish and harvest enough wild edible foods on which to live comfortably. Singer eventually constructed a masted raft on which he could sail to the nearest port for supplies. Singer's wife obtained some seeds and planted a garden, providing fresh vegetables to accompany the bounty they harvested from the sea. Singer salvaged timbers from the wrecked ship, built a frame house, and fashioned some furniture. Truly, Singer thought, they had discovered an Eden, and each day brought renewed evidence that his decision to remain on the island was the correct one.

During one of their beachcombing forays, the Singer children found some old coins lying in the sand not far from the house. When Singer saw the coins, he judged them to be of Spanish origin and made of pure gold. Thinking there might be more coins around, Singer and his children returned to the site and dug up a rotted wooden cask containing approximately $80,000 in coins as well as several pieces of well-crafted jewelry. Singer assumed the cask had been buried on the beach by pirates who never returned to collect it.

Using some of the Spanish coins, Singer purchased a large herd of cattle, had them shipped to the island, and turned them loose to graze on the rich grasses that grew there. As Singer prospered in the cattle business, he and his children continued to find other buried pirate treasures, and over time, the family amassed a great fortune in gold and silver coins and jewelry.

Selecting a large sand dune about a half mile from his house as his "bank," Singer buried his wealth, digging it up and using portions of it as needed. Singer jokingly referred to his treasure dune as "Money Hill" and over the years continued to add newly discovered coins to the cache.

When the War Between The States broke out in 1861, warships of the northern forces were often seen patrolling the waters on the horizon. Concerned that Yankee forces might land on the island and confiscate possessions and cattle, Singer collected all of his valuables, transported them to Money Hill, and buried them with the rest of his wealth. It has been estimated that Singer concealed well over $100,000 worth of gold and silver coins and jewelry at this site. A second cask, filled with a smaller amount of coins, was carried to a different part of the island and buried at a place described only as being "near two small oaks."

Within just a few days, the officers of the Yankee warships became aware of the abundance of cattle on Padre Island. Experiencing shortages of fresh meat, they made several trips to Singer's ranch to procure some. Initially they purchased cattle from the rancher, but as funds grew low, they resorted to confiscating them. Singer became increasingly nervous about the all too frequent visits of the sailors and finally moved the family to the mainland to wait out the war.

Four years later, when the war ended, the Singers returned to the island only to find their home and property had been destroyed. Part of the destruction was by the sailors who occupied the island. They had torn down the frame house and used the timbers for firewood. Cooking pits had been dug throughout the yard, and no cattle could be found anywhere.

Another kind of disaster had struck the island in Singer's absence as well. A tremendous hurricane a year earlier had ravaged Padre Island, altering the terrain for miles around. In some places, there were bays where none existed before. In other areas, prominent sand dunes had been completely leveled.

When John Singer and his oldest son made a trek to Money Hill to recover their buried wealth, the dune was not to be found! The terrain had been changed so dramatically that Singer had trouble getting his bearings. A subsequent trip to the second cache near the two oaks was equally discouraging; the trees had vanished and the shoreline was entirely unrecognizable.

Singer and his family chose once again to remain on Padre Island. He eventually restocked the area with cattle and continued to operate the ranch until his death in 1877. From the time he returned to the island, Singer passionately pursued his search for the lost treasure. Because he was unable to relocate any of it, and because he failed to make any profit from the renewed ranching enterprise, his brother Isaac had to subsidize him for the last few years of his life.

At one time a very wealthy man, John Singer was nearly a pauper when he passed away in 1877. Most of Padre Island has been designated by the federal government as a National Seashore, and the Singer homesite is a local tourist attraction. His treasure, worth well over a million dollars today, is still lost in the sand somewhere nearby.

The Curse of the Neches River Treasure

There are so many stories of lost treasure supposedly buried by the famous pirate Jean Laffite that they could scarcely fit in a single book. Many are undoubtedly true, but as the reputation and mystique of the colorful buccaneer grew, so did the number and kinds of tales told about him, and the more they were repeated, the more fantastic they became.

Laffite himself cultivated this mystique. An elusive, sly, enterprising adventurer, he was also a highly skilled self-promoter who understood the value of a reputation as a notorious and feared freebooter. Though most certainly a real person, Laffite's life is shrouded in mystery. No one knows exactly where he came from or where he went when he abandoned pirating. Some say he retired to the Yucatán in Mexico and others offer evidence he passed away in St. Louis. In death as in life, Laffite confounded and confused.

Woven among the tales of Laffite's buried treasures are numerous stories of hauntings and curses. Almost as many people have claimed to have seen Laffite's ghost as have claimed to possess a map to one of his treasures.

Particularly intriguing is a tale about one of Laffite's buried caches and a curse said to have been placed on the site. Any who attempted to remove the treasure were to be stricken, and many were—some to death.

The exact date is uncertain, but sometime in 1820, Jean Laffite and his crew piloted a treasure-laden ship to a point near where the Neches River enters the secluded bay of Port Arthur near the Texas–Louisiana border. Steering the vessel close to shore, Laffite selected a spot in which to conceal several chests filled with coins and jewels recently taken from a Spanish ship on its way from Mexico to Cuba. Laffite hurried his men along for he was aware of pursuit by a second Spanish galleon, its captain intent on recovering the treasure and taking revenge on the pirates.

Laffite's ship was moored to the shore by a long heavy iron chain secured to a stout tree near the river. The pirate leader ordered his men to bury the chests in the shadow of the tree.

As the pirates were filling the hole, the pursuing Spanish vessel appeared in the bay heading toward them. No sooner had Laffite ordered his men back on board than he turned toward the site of the buried treasure and placed a curse, vowing that anyone unworthy to reclaim the cache would be stricken with unnamed horrors. Returning to the ship, the pirates primed the cannons, hoisted the sails, and quickly loosed the heavy chain, letting it drop into the water. The other end of the chain was still attached to the tree.

As Laffite's vessel moved out into the bay, the pirates challenged the Spanish galleon, and for over an hour, the two ships battled. The bay resounded with cannon fire and the cheers and shouts of sailors and buccaneers. Reeling from the superior fire power of the Spaniards, the pirate ship managed to elude the pursuing vessel and escape into the Gulf of Mexico. The relief of the escape was short-lived, however, for the Spanish ship continued pursuit and was rapidly closing in. About two miles offshore, Laffite's ship took several direct cannon hits and sank.

Miraculously, Laffite escaped. It is not known whether he stayed on shore when the pirate vessel sailed into the bay or whether he managed to elude being plucked from the water by the Spaniards, but within only a few weeks he was again sailing the gulf, plundering Spanish vessels with a fury unlike anything seen before or since. Legend claims he never recovered the Neches River treasure.

Many years later, when Laffite was just a memory in the minds of Gulf Coast residents, a curious map surfaced, a crudely-constructed map containing the description of the chaining of the pirate vessel to the tree, of the battle with the Spaniards, and of burying millions of dollars' worth of Spanish gold coins and jewels. Though very inexpertly drawn, the map was clear to anyone familiar with the territory: the alleged treasure cache was hidden near the mouth of the Neches River.

The map somehow came into the possession of a Mexican peasant shortly after the Civil War. According to the man's widow, he followed the directions to the treasure, found the tree with the heavy chain still attached, and started digging. No one knows what he found, for the man returned home the following day in a state of shock and unable to speak. Whatever happened to him during his attempt to recover the treasure caused him to lose his voice, and he was unable to explain what transpired. Within a week, he was dead from unknown causes.

Some years later, the Mexican's widow passed the map on to an Anglo neighbor who lived nearby. The man, a farmer with a small family, got excited at the prospect of recovering a treasure of the famous Jean Laffite and he began to make plans to journey to the mouth of the Neches River. The Mexican woman didn't tell him of the fate that had befallen her husband.

The farmer made a trip to the treasure site described on the map. Like the Mexican before him, he found the tree and the chain and began to excavate. After digging about two feet down, the man suddenly jerked upright as if seized by something unseen. He flailed his arms and grasped at his throat as if trying to ward off a strangulation. With great difficulty, the farmer extricated himself from the hole and returned to his home. Like the unfortunate Mexican who preceded him to the treasure site, the farmer lost his powers of speech and was dead before a week passed. His belongings, including the treasure map, were stored away and forgotten.

Years later, the farmer's widow cleaned out many of her late husband's belongings and gave them to a neighbor named Meredith who had recently moved to the area. The widow explained about the old map and told the stories of the two men who were apparently victims of the pirate's curse. Undaunted by the tale, Meredith decided to try to recover the treasure and jokingly referred to the old map as "the widow maker." After his experience in attempting to retrieve the long-buried pirate cache, however, Meredith never joked about the subject again for as long as he lived.

Meredith did not believe in hauntings and curses and was skeptical of the tale related by the widow. He enlisted a partner to accompany him on his search, an old friend named Clawson, and together the two arrived at the exact location indicated on the map.

Almost at once, Meredith and Clawson found the tree near the bank of the river with the heavy chain still attached. Next to the tree was a shallow cavity in the ground, obviously where someone had previously dug. Nearby were a badly rusted shovel and pickaxe.

Meredith and Clawson began to excavate at the site of the cavity, and they had removed about three feet of soil when they encountered a skeleton, carefully laid out and wrapped in what had once been a canvas sail. The metal buttons and buckles and the remains of leather boots suggested it was a pirate's skeleton. Very carefully, the two men removed the bones, intending to rebury them when they were done.

As the hole deepened, Meredith and Clawson, tired, decided to alternate the digging chores. After a stint in the hole, Meredith climbed to the top and leaned against the tree for some rest while Clawson took a turn. He was on the point of falling asleep when he was jarred awake by Clawson's shrieks. Meredith saw a wide-eyed Clawson scrambling frantically out of the deep hole. He looked as if he had aged twenty years, and his eyes seemed on the verge of popping out of his head.

Grabbing Meredith, the obviously horrified Clawson implored him to leave the place immediately. Meredith tried to look in the pit to see what his partner had seen, but Clawson held his friend and prevented him from approaching the hole. Drawing Meredith's face close to his, the quivering Clawson told him he had just stared into the depths of hell and seen all its horrors.

Clawson's terror was so overwhelming and his hold on Meredith so unyielding that there was nothing to do but leave the place at once. The men literally ran down the trail away from the site, abandoning all their tools. When they got home, the still-frightened Clawson begged his friend Meredith never to return to the site of the pirate treasure.

In spite of Clawson's warnings, Meredith decided weeks later to go back to retrieve his tools. Cautiously approaching the tree and the pit, he saw the skeleton was still lying where he and Clawson placed it. The hole had been partially filled with mud as a result of recent rains. Meredith carefully replaced the skeleton in the hole and covered it up. He gathered his tools and never returned to the site for as long as he lived.

Clawson never completely recovered from his experience, although he did not die like the others who were involved in excavating the treasure site. For the rest of his life, Clawson jumped in terror at the merest sound or sudden movement, and his body trembled as if he were in a constant state of terror. He eventually moved to Beaumont, and it was there Meredith ran into him one day several years later. Meredith tried once again to get his friend to describe what he had seen in the treasure pit years ago, but Clawson refused to discuss it and pleaded with Meredith never to ask him again.

Whatever the Mexican peasant, the farmer, and Clawson saw in the treasure pit will probably never be known. The suggestion of a curse on this buried cache has added another dimension to the mysteries associated with the complex and elusive pirate, Jean Laffite.

The Shipwrecks on Deer Island

September is a difficult month for those who sail the Gulf of Mexico. Storms are common, and they often arise without warning.

It was one such September in 1820 that three privateers sailed north toward Galveston Island after a series of successful raids on Spanish treasure ships plying the waters between the Yucatán and Cuba. The heavy and growing storm overtook them as they raced northward, and stiff winds flailed the three craft unmercifully while the rough seas threatened to capsize them.

As the captains began to fear they might not survive to see land again, Galveston Island was sighted, and all three vessels sailed for that welcome sanctuary. The ships' pilots had hoped to make the shallow waters of the Sabine River, but it was too far away to take the chance. With the storm's fury growing every minute, it was Galveston Island or nothing.

The ships sailed through a narrow channel and around a point, seeking the lee side of the island. Within minutes, the pirates could make out the lights of Campeche, a rough-and-tumble pirate stronghold. The town was not faring well in the storm, and several of the wooden frame shacks had blown down. As the full force of the storm hit the settlement, roads turned into rivers of mud, and those homes and businesses that stood were eventually flattened. The only structures to survive the onslaught of the storm were the pier and a stone warehouse close to the shore.

The pirates dropped anchor in Campeche harbor and braved the rough waters in rowboats to reach shore. In their haste to abandon the ships, the pirates didn't take time to batten them down so they could ride out the storm at anchor. No crew members remained on board, and none of the rich cargo of gold and silver bars was unloaded. The pirates apparently decided to wait out the storm in the warehouse and return to their boats the next day.

Inside the warehouse, the pirates discovered that most of their shorebound compatriots had also sought shelter in the stout building, converting it into a makeshift tavern. The Campeche residents had already consumed an impressive amount of rum by the time the storm-harried sailors arrived, and they invited their fellows to join them.

As the night wore on, the pirates got drunk and were oblivious to what was transpiring in the harbor. All three vessels broke loose from their moorings, drifted into West Bay, and slammed up against North Deer Island, one of three large sandy knolls projecting above the level of the waters. All three craft broke open on impact and sank into the soft mud.

Two days later, when the pirates recovered from their debauches and discovered the vessels were missing, they searched for them. Believing the winds had remained constantly out of the south during the storm, the pirates looked to the north, not in the actual direction the vessels were blown. They sailed up and down the coast north of Campeche for weeks, and didn't find the ships. The search was eventually called off, and the three treasure-laden pirate vessels were soon forgotten.

The Deer Islands were not often frequented by people of the Galveston Island area. They offered nothing that attracted settlement and remained unpopulated and seldom visited. Over time, drifting sands covered most of the three ships that lay undisturbed on the submerged mud flats for so many years.

As time passed and Galveston grew and prospered, more and more people used the bay for fishing and other kinds of recreation. While the Deer Islands were nothing more than sandy bumps just above water level between Galveston Island and the mainland, the adjacent area became a favored fishing site for many. Sometime in the 1950s, a lone fisherman was trying his luck near the north shore of North Deer Island when he was caught by a sudden storm. Rather than try to outrun it back to the mainland, the fisherman decided to seek shelter on the island. Securing his boat and crouching under a low-growing tree near the shore, he watched as the winds and waves tormented the island. Several times when the wind was blowing from the island northward toward the bay, he caught momentary glimpses of a row of cannons several yards offshore as the shallow mudbanks were temporarily exposed.

When the storm abated, the fisherman walked out to the edge of the mud flats and could barely discern the outlines of three ships lying just below the surface of the water. He tried to wade out to the sunken boats to inspect them, but had problems with sinking into the soft bottom. When he tried to steer his own boat into the area, he found the water far too shallow. He returned to the mainland to organize an expedition to return to the sunken vessels, but on a subsequent trip to North Deer Island, he couldn't find them. Cursing himself for not taking compass bearings on his location, the fisherman searched the area for several days but without success.

Several times since then, occupants of fishing boats and pilots of low-flying aircraft have reported seeing one to three submerged vessels just off the northern shore of North Deer Island. Several organized searches have been made, but the submerged vessels have eluded the treasure hunters.

In 1970, a man carrying a bar of silver entered a small jewelry shop in downtown Houston and offered to sell it to the proprietor. The owner of the shop specialized in custom-made handcrafted jewelry of gold, silver, and semi-precious stones. Most of what he sold he made himself, but he also carried some merchandise on consignment.

After analyzing the bar of silver and determining it was the purest he had ever seen, the jeweler asked his visitor where he had gotten it. The man, behaving somewhat secretively, claimed he found the bar, along with several others, many years earlier in the mud flats just north of North Deer Island. He said he at first believed the bars were lead but learned only recently that they were high-grade silver.

The jeweler purchased the bar and inquired if the man would care to sell him the rest. Without answering, he scurried out the door. He was never seen again.

The jeweler told the story to a friend who, using the vague directions that were provided, went to the approximate location of the find at North Deer Island. He found that much of the area described by the jeweler had been disrupted and displaced during construction of the Intracoastal Waterway. The mud flats, so often mentioned by those who reported seeing the sunken ships, had been dredged to accommodate a deep ship channel. Huge mechanical shovels have scooped up mud and sand by the ton and deposited it in a series of spoils banks north of the waterway. Undoubtedly, broken and rotted portions of the three sunken ships, along with the treasure cargo, were removed and reburied a short distance away.

Though the exact amount of treasure carried by the three pirate vessels in 1820 is unknown, researchers suggest that several million dollars' worth of gold, silver, and jewelry, in addition to other valuable artifacts, went down with the ships.

The Treasure of Matagorda Bay

In the early 1920s, a very old man roamed the streets of New York City begging for handouts and sleeping in dark alleys. The man, whose name was Robinson, had documents proving he was over a hundred years old. Robinson was sickly and near the point of death when he was discovered by a man named William Selkirk, a wealthy businessman known for his contributions to charitable causes.

Selkirk immediately made arrangements for the sick old man to be moved into his mansion, and obtained a nurse to provide around-the-clock care. Though the environment of the Selkirk mansion was far better than the rough streets on which he had lived for so many years, the old man was diagnosed as having double pneumonia and given only a few days to live.

One evening, the dying man called for Selkirk, who came and sat by his bedside. Having great difficulty speaking, Robinson voiced his gratitude to the businessman for helping him and told him he wanted to give him a gift. He was weak and shaky and his body wracked with painful fits of coughing, but the old man managed to reach into a tattered pouch he owned, withdraw a rolled-up parchment, and hand it to Selkirk. The businessman carefully unrolled the obviously very old and delicate parchment and saw it was a map of considerable age. The map purported to show the location of a fantastic buried treasure near where the Colorado River emptied into Matagorda Bay. As Selkirk gazed at the map, the old man told an amazing tale.

Robinson claimed to have been a pirate in his youth, serving under a ruthless ship captain who in turn received his orders from Jean Laffite. Working as a cabin boy and sailor, he went along on many raids on Spanish treasure ships, seizing cargos of gold, silver, and jewels. As a result of a series of successful raids, Robinson's captain soon gained notoriety as one of the bloodiest and cruelest to ply the Gulf of Mexico, and the Spanish government doubled its efforts to apprehend the menace and put him out of business.

One morning after a successful raid on a Spanish treasure ship near Vera Cruz, the rising sun found the pirate vessel moored on the Gulf side of Matagorda Peninsula, not far from the narrow opening into Matagorda Bay.

A lookout high on the mainmast spotted a Spanish warship bearing down on them from the south. Sails were hoisted, and the outlaw ship sailed into the bay. The pirate captain, aware that the Spanish warship had a deeper draft than his own, decided to seek the shelter of the Colorado River. He believed his ship could find safety several miles up the river while the larger and heavier Spanish boat would mire itself on the shallow bottom.

The captain, however, was not aware of recent large silt deposits at the mouth of the river resulting from heavy rains far inland. As the pirate ship negotiated the turn into the river's current, it ran aground.

The Spanish ship was still some distance away, and as the captain commanded some of his men to ready the cannons for battle, he ordered Robinson and two other sailors to accompany him to shore to bury the treasure.

The three sailors filled a large wooden chest with gold and silver coins and valuable jewels and lugged it to shore. Selecting the highest point for several miles around, the captain ordered the sailors to drag the chest to the top and bury it. Standing on the promontory, the captain named it Gold Point and made a detailed sketch of the area on a large parchment, noting landmarks and compass readings. When he finished, the captain rolled the parchment, placed it in a leather container, and handed it to Robinson for safekeeping. Then the captain ordered the group back to the ship to help prepare for the attack from the Spaniards.

The assault came early the next morning. At sunrise, the Spanish warship opened fire, and within minutes, the pirate vessel was destroyed. The captain, as well as Robinson's two fellow sailors, were killed during the initial fusillade. Robinson panicked, jumped ship, waded to shore, and escaped deep into the mainland. He was now the only man alive who knew the exact location of the buried treasure of Gold Point.

In his haste to escape, Robinson did not consider stopping and retrieving any of the buried treasure, but he had the parchment map still clutched in his hands. He didn't stop until he had put several miles between himself and the shoreline.

Knowing the Spanish government had placed a bounty on the heads of Gulf Coast pirates, Robinson decided not to return to his former haunts until the threat of capture and execution diminished. He spent the next several years wandering through Texas, and eventually made his way to California, where he remained for several decades. His life was such that he was never able to return to recover any of the buried treasure at the mouth of the Colorado River at Matagorda Bay, but he always carried the parchment with him, hoping someday to be able to return.

As a very old man, Robinson came to New York City. Infirm and unable to find work, he survived by begging for handouts. His health grew worse, and it was in this condition that Selkirk found him.

William Selkirk was fascinated by the old pirate's tale and vowed to use the map to try to recover the treasure. Within weeks, the businessman took the long journey to the Texas Gulf Coast. When he arrived at Matagorda Bay, he fell in love with the area and purchased six thousand acres of prime farming and grazing land, acreage that included the promontory on which the treasure chest was supposedly buried.

Selkirk made several casual attempts to locate the treasure, but he soon discovered his passion was raising cattle and farming. He gradually lost interest in the cache.

Selkirk hired a man named George Ellis to manage his ranch for him, and several years later when the entrepreneur decided to return to New York, he made Ellis responsible for the management of his Texas properties. Ellis remained as caretaker for the Selkirk enterprises along the Gulf Coast for the next forty years.

From time to time, men would arrive at the Selkirk Ranch requesting permission to dig for treasure. Ellis, who knew nothing of the tale of the Gold Point treasure cache, generally allowed treasure hunters to dig in the area since it did not disturb the normal ranch operations.

One day in the early 1950s, a group of treasure hunters from Bay City arrived at the ranch headquarters and asked Ellis to guide them to Gold Point. Ellis demurred, but the men were insistent, finally offering to pay him well for his efforts. Not one to turn down an easy payday, Ellis agreed.

Using an old map they claimed had been found between the pages of a book at some university library, the treasure hunters, along with Ellis, arrived at Gold Point, and the men excavated several holes near the top. Ellis, caught up in the fever of the search for treasure, grabbed a shovel and started to dig a hole himself.

After removing two to three feet of topsoil, Ellis's spade struck something solid. Looking about to see that no one was watching him, he scraped away some of the loose dirt and looked down onto the top of a large wooden chest fitted with thick metal bindings and fittings. Ellis decided not to share his discovery with the treasure hunters. Instead, he casually filled a portion of the hole and began digging another one nearby.

Presently, the men decided to stop for the day. Ellis escorted them from the Selkirk property and watched as they drove away. Ellis returned to the ranch house, intending to return to Gold Point the next morning and recover the treasure chest.

The next day was to provide an unexpected surprise for the ranch manager. Arriving at Gold Point just moments after sunup, Ellis walked straight to where he had dug the previous afternoon. As he approached the hole, he detected a slight difference. He had partially filled it the previous day, but this morning it looked as though fresh dirt had been removed and deposited around the margins of the excavation. Peering into the hole, Ellis stared at a rectangular space at the bottom, a space from which a large chest had obviously been removed.

The treasure hunters had apparently suspected Ellis of finding something and had returned in the middle of the night.

What became of the chest and its rich contents has never been revealed. For many years, George Ellis told the story of how he was merely a spade-length from a great fortune in gold and silver and let it get away.

East Texas Piney Woods

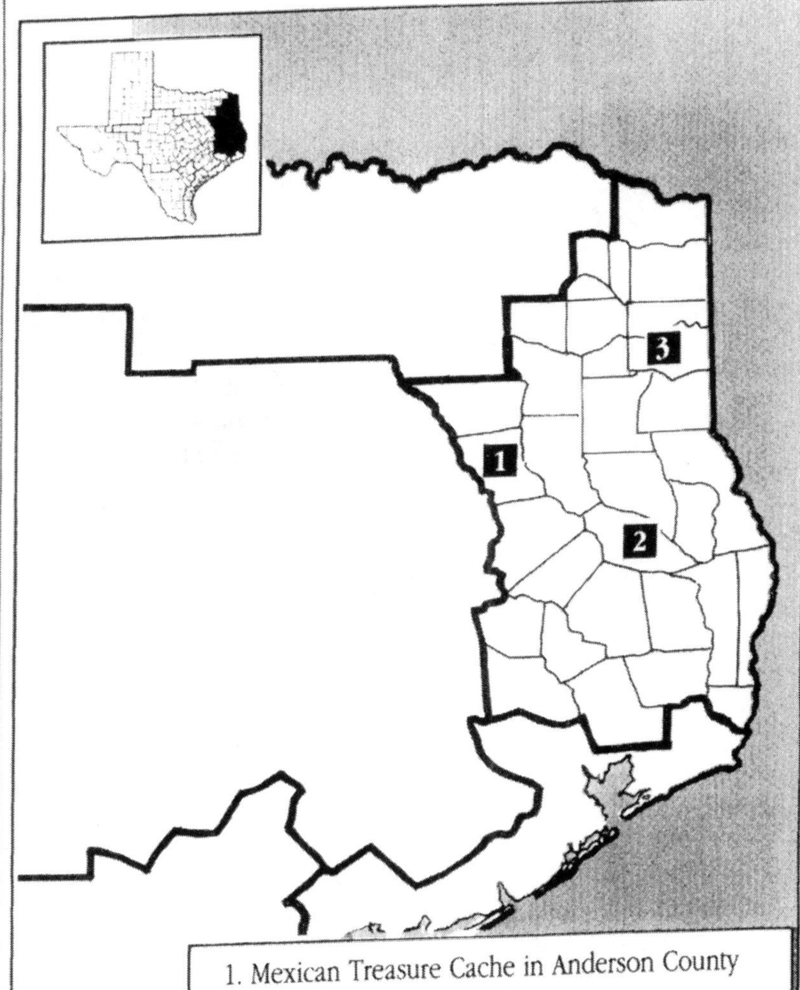

1. Mexican Treasure Cache in Anderson County
2. The Biloxi Creek Treasure
3. The Hendricks Lake Treasure

Mexican Treasure Cache in Anderson County

Not far from the town of Elkhart in Anderson County is the site of the old Pilgrim Community. Little remains of this pre–Civil War settlement save for some dim memories of an old church and its graveyard. Pilgrim Church was reputed to be the first Protestant church in the state of Texas.

According to area legend, a great fortune in Mexican gold coins, gold bars, and jewels lies buried somewhere near the location of the old church. The legend has some basis in fact, but the buried wealth has eluded searchers for generations.

This story of buried treasure has its origin deep in the heart of Mexico, where Felicia Cortez, daughter of a wealthy and powerful landowner and politico, was banished from her homeland and sent north to the Mission of San Francisco de las Tejas near the Neches River in East Texas. The mission had been established many years earlier to convert and serve the local Indians. A convent had been added, and about a dozen nuns were in residence. It was to this convent that Felicia Cortez was sent.

Details of the banishment of Señorita Cortez are sketchy, but stories revolve around her having disgraced her family by falling in love with a peasant. After she was sent away, the peasant was allegedly tied to a corral fence and beaten to death.

The elder Cortez provided his daughter with a chest of jewels which were to finance the journey northward to the mission. Any remaining jewels were to be donated to the church on arrival.

On the evening before her departure, Felicia Cortez took enough of her father's gold bars and coins to load down five burros. Felicia had little interest in living in a convent and entertained the idea of becoming a wealthy landowner in Texas. She anticipated building a fine home, overseeing some rich land, and raising blooded horses. She intended to become an influential force in the new lands to the north much as her father was deep in Mexico.

Felicia left early the next morning with five faithful servants and her new wealth.

The journey northward was long, tiring, and uneventful. Day after day, the pack train trudged across the endless expanse of desert and shrub. After several weeks, the small party crossed the Rio Grande near present-day Laredo and continued northeast for many more days, crossing the Nueces, San Antonio, Guadalupe, Colorado, and Trinity Rivers. Much of the road traveled by the Cortez party paralleled *el camino real,* the ancient "royal road" traveled by the first Spaniards in the region.

Their path would take them near the old mission to which Felicia was consigned, but the spirited young girl was more interested in the fertile land of the Trinity and Neches River bottoms.

Shortly after crossing the Trinity, Señorita Cortez ordered her servants to establish a camp. The following morning, she told them, they would begin to search the area for a suitable place in which to settle and build a fine house.

Around midafternoon, the party made a temporary camp just a short distance from the trail. Tired from many weeks of travel, the group napped in the warmth of the Texas sun.

While they were sleeping, the camp was suddenly attacked by a band of Indians. Emerging from the adjacent woods, the screaming attackers loosed dozens of arrows into the party of Mexicans. One of the servants was killed immediately by an arrow through his neck.

The remaining servants returned fire with their muskets and succeeded in driving the Indians back into the woods. As the savages readied for another assault on the small party, the Mexicans gathered nearby logs and rocks and constructed a crude fortification. As they were engaged in this activity, Felicia Cortez frantically searched for a place to hide her fortune.

Once again the Indians attacked, and once again they were repelled. Two Indians were killed, and one of the Mexicans was severely wounded.

When the Indians retreated a second time, Felicia ordered one of the servants to help her bury her fortune near the edge of the campground. Hastily, the two scooped out a shallow trench into which they dropped the gold and jewels. Just as they were covering the treasure with dirt and forest debris, the Indians attacked for the third time.

The servant who was helping Felicia rushed to the aid of his fellows, and when he left, the young girl escaped into the nearby forest, fearing that her small force of men would not be sufficient to hold out against the large force of Indians.

As her servants perished in this third and final attack, Felicia raced through the dense forest. She fled in the general direction of the mission.

After three days in the forest, Señorita Cortez arrived at the Mission of San Francisco de las Tejas. Her clothes were torn and filthy, and she bled from many cuts. She was nearly out of her mind with fright.

For several months, Felicia either could not bring herself to speak of the treasure she had buried at the fateful campground or she had blotted it out of her mind. Feeling safe and secure at the mission under the protection and care of the doting nuns, she gradually recovered from her ordeal.

Some who have studied the case of Felicia Cortez believe she planned to stay at the mission until she regained her health and then return to the camp, recover her buried treasure, and proceed with her plans to establish a fine ranch in the area. Others believe she went insane during the attack by the Indians and completely forgot everything that happened, including the existence of the treasure.

Though her actual motive will likely never be known, the fact is that Felicia Cortez lived at the mission for several years and eventually entered the order of nuns with whom she spent her days. It has been suggested that she found true happiness in the embrace of the Lord and that she preferred to perform His work rather than to heed the call of the buried wealth some few miles to the southwest.

Many years passed, and eventually Sister Felicia returned to Mexico where she was reunited with her family. She remained a nun until she grew very old and finally passed away. Before she died, however, Sister Felicia made a startling revelation. She confided to relatives the existence of the buried treasure deep in the pine forests along an old trail in far away East Texas. She sketched a crude map and provided details of the treasure and its location. The information was written down, stored with other family possessions, and eventually forgotten.

Years later, some descendants of the Cortez family found the maps and accompanying descriptions while rummaging among items stored away in old trunks. The documents were examined, and the old story of the Cortez treasure told among family members was heard in a different light. A search party was organized to travel to the alleged site and recover the gold coins, bars, and jewels and return them to the family coffers.

Near the turn of the century, the party arrived in the region where the Cortez treasure was allegedly buried. They saw with dismay that this area, once wild and unsettled, was now the location of farms and homesteads. Hostile Indians were no longer a threat, but the searchers now had to cope with the curious eyes of the many settlers who populated the region.

Within sight of the approximate location described by Felicia Cortez were the Pilgrim Church, a graveyard, and a small community.

With the passing of the years, many of the landmarks indicated in Felicia Cortez's description of the treasure site had been obliterated by farming and settlement activity. The search party did find what they believed to be the site of the fateful campground and excavated several likely areas.

They searched and dug and continued to discuss and disagree on landmarks and directions for several days. Eventually the frustrated and disheartened group packed up and left, never to return.

By now, the story of the buried Mexican cache of gold and jewels had circulated far and wide through East Texas, and soon others came in search of the buried wealth. Maps were produced and holes were dug, but no fortune was ever found.

In recent years, residents of the area have reported seeing a ghost moving about the old graveyard located in the old Pilgrim community. The ghost is clad in the garb of a nun, and it is believed to be the spirit of Felicia Cortez.

Some claim that the ghost of Felicia Cortez is guarding the great fortune buried beneath the ground. Many believe that the graveyard is the actual site of the campground in which the fortune was buried well over 150 years ago.

The Biloxi Creek Treasure

Texas was the setting for much economic and social turbulence during the years just after the War Between the States. Because much of the state was thinly populated, violators of law and order often sought refuge in remote rural areas far from the inquisitive eyes of law enforcement officials.

Adding to this lawlessness were many returning soldiers who discovered that farming and ranching did not provide the excitement they knew in the war. Finding the agrarian life boring and not to their liking any longer, many of these men continued to live by their wits—and by their guns.

One such gang of men, partly returning soldiers and partly local ne'er-do-wells, found the deep, thick pine woods of Angelina County to their liking. Following raids throughout the countryside in which they indulged in robbery and sometimes murder, these marauders retreated to the cabin of a farmer named Squires. Squires had lived here for several years with his wife and young child. Squires's wife, somewhat younger than he and quite comely, became housekeeper and cook for the gang.

The Squires's cabin was on the west bank of Biloxi Creek, a permanent stream which bisected a part of the county, and the site was somewhat isolated, with the nearest neighbor living several miles away. The outlaw gang felt safe and secure at the Squires farm and made it their regular hide-out.

Although farmer Squires never participated in any of the robberies and killings, he was considered a member of the gang because he let the outlaws congregate at his cabin. In turn, the outlaws trusted Squires enough to have him cache the take from their many holdups. Gold, money, and jewelry were turned over to Squires after raids, and he would add it to the growing store of wealth buried somewhere on his property.

At first, Squires was delighted with his relationship with the outlaws, for they paid him well. As time passed, however, and the outlaws became more violent, Squires came to fear them and dreaded their arrival at his farm.

With one successful robbery after another, the outlaws became more and more brazen and soon expanded their range of depredations over a wider territory. Sometimes they would be gone for weeks, committing robberies as far away as San Antonio, Houston, and Fort Worth. They soon added horse stealing to their criminal repertoire and would often arrive at the Squires farm with as many as a hundred horses in tow.

Around midnight one evening, the gang rode up to the cabin in a foul mood. A bank robbery attempt in an adjacent county had been unsuccessful, and the outlaws had been driven from the community at gunpoint by irate citizens. The outlaws' dispositions were not improved by having ridden all the way back to the Squires farm in a driving rainstorm.

The men had begun drinking on their way back, and by the time they arrived, they were all drunk and surly.

When they stormed into the cabin, they found Squires and his wife asleep. The outlaws pulled them out of bed, cursing and yelling at them, and ordered Squires's wife to cook them some dinner. As she retreated to the kitchen, they began to shove the farmer around and shoot holes in the roof of the cabin so that rain leaked through onto the dirt floor.

The outlaws kept drinking and soon started quarreling with one another. Squires was pleased at this turn of events, for it meant that the outlaws temporarily forgot him and left him alone.

Soon some gang members began to demand their share of the accumulated loot. More arguing ensued, and it was eventually agreed that the cache should be retrieved and divided. They ordered Squires to go dig it up and bring it into the cabin.

Squires, fearful of the outlaws yet not wanting to go out into the storm to dig up the treasure, argued against it, telling them that the loot was buried in the yard and it would wait until morning. The outlaws told Squires they didn't want to wait and demanded he retrieve it immediately. Squires refused angrily and told them they were too drunk to count and divide the wealth.

The outlaws were belligerent and threatening. Seeing that things were getting out of hand, Squires slammed open the cabin door and bolted outside. Several of the drunken outlaws ran out onto the porch and fired their guns at the fleeing figure. By the time the smoke cleared, Squires lay dead on the muddy ground. A small stream of water swirled about his prone body, mixing with the blood that poured from a dozen bullet holes.

As the outlaws went out into the storm to examine Squires, the farmer's wife grabbed the child and ran into the woods. She ran for miles in the rain, eventually arriving at the cabin of some neighbors named Renfro. There she told the story of the outlaws and what they did to her husband.

The outlaws, unable to find the buried treasure and worried that the woman would bring the sheriff in the morning, packed up and fled from the area, never to be heard of again.

Years passed, and the story of the incident at Squires's cabin and the buried treasure cache became only a dim memory among a few of the old-timers in Angelina County. Nearly a generation had passed since the death of Squires when a man named Marion Grimes acquired the old farm. Grimes built a new cabin, tilled the land, and raised some cattle. All in all, he found the place quite pleasant and livable.

One night while sleeping in his new cabin, Grimes had a strange dream wherein a man he had never seen before took him by the hand and led him far out into the yard. The figure pointed to a spot on the ground and said, "Dig here! A lot of money is buried at this spot." Grimes awoke with a start to find himself standing over the exact spot in the yard that he had seen in his dream.

Understandably frightened, Grimes hitched a pair of horses to a wagon and fled to the nearest town, a settlement called Flournoy. He told the story of his strange experience to several Flournoy citizens, and all of them agreed that the man in the dream matched a description of farmer Squires.

Grimes, believing that the old farm was haunted, lost interest in his holdings, sold the property shortly thereafter, and soon left the area permanently.

Many more years passed, and the forest soon encroached upon and gradually covered the old Squires farm. There are a few citizens in the area who claim to know where the cabin once stood, but they won't go into the woods because of poisonous snakes and the dense tangle of undergrowth. A forestry products company now owns the land, and "No Trespassing" signs have been posted to discourage searchers.

But somewhere beneath the tangled briars and shadowing pines along the west bank of Biloxi Creek may lie one of the richest treasure caches ever to exist in Texas.

The Hendricks Lake Treasure

One of the best known lost treasures in East Texas is that associated with the hurried dumping of six wagons into the murky waters of Hendricks Lake near the town of Longview in Harrison County. Abundant evidence exists to support the validity of the tale, and on different occasions, silver ingots and fragments of freight wagons a century-and-a-half old were actually retrieved from the lake bottom.

The story has its beginnings in 1816, and one of the principals is the notorious pirate, Jean Laffite, around whom many a tale of stolen, lost, and buried treasure has been woven. Laffite, the Gentleman Pirate of the Gulf Coast, was well known for his looting of trading and sailing vessels throughout the Gulf of Mexico. Headquartered on Galveston Island, Laffite dominated the northern shore of the Gulf for many years.

Among his favorite targets for raiding were the Spanish galleons which transported gold and silver from the Americas to Spain. His raids on Spanish vessels generated pursuit and harassment from Mexican and Spanish authorities to the extent that Laffite was forced to vacate his Galveston Island sanctuary and seek refuge 150 miles to the southwest at Corpus Christi Bay. From this new vantage point, Laffite pursued his piracy and continued to prey on the rich, poorly armed, undermanned Spanish ships.

In the spring of 1816, the *Santa Rosa,* sailing under the Spanish flag, was carrying over $2 million in silver ingots to Havana when it was blown off course by a severe storm and forced to take refuge in Matagorda Bay, some ninety miles up the coast from Corpus Christi. The ingots were destined for the Spanish treasury at Madrid, but fate decreed that they would never arrive there.

After two days at anchor in the protected bay, the captain of the *Santa Rosa* decided the storm had abated enough to continue the voyage. As the crew was setting the sails, a small armada led by Laffite swarmed into the bay and attacked. Caught by surprise and considerably outnumbered, the *Santa Rosa* surrendered to the Gentleman Pirate.

Each recent seizure by Laffite had been followed immediately by an organized pursuit. Believing it was only a matter of a few days until word spread of the attack and pillage of the *Santa Rosa,* Laffite decided it would be prudent to rid himself of the tremendous haul of silver before Mexican and Spanish authorities descended on his refuge.

Because Laffite stayed only a step or two ahead of pursuit and because he believed his days of piracy in the area were numbered, he elected to have the silver taken to St. Louis where it was to be stored with other booty he had stolen over the years. Laffite assigned one of his accomplices, a surly brute named Gaspar Trammel, to deliver the silver to the bustling city on the Mississippi River. Trammel owned a freight line that made regular runs from the Texas coast to St. Louis on a trail that has come to be known as the Trammel Trace. Trammel loaded the silver onto six wagons and, in the company of several other wagons carrying goods and supplies, began the long journey to the northeast.

The wagon train had covered a bit over two hundred miles when Trammel decided to set up camp next to a small lake fed by the headwaters of the Sabine River. The teamsters and draft animals were in need of rest, and as water and game were plentiful in the region, it seemed an ideal site. As the drivers were unhitching the animals, a scout rode into the camp and told the men a large contingent of Mexican soldiers was no more than a mile behind them and approaching rapidly.

Not wishing to be caught with the six wagonloads of stolen silver ingots, Trammel ordered his head driver, a man named Robert Dawson, to roll them into the lake. Moments later, as the Trammel party was preparing to flee, the Mexican troops arrived and attacked, killing Trammel and most of his drivers. Dawson and two others managed to escape into the dense forest surrounding the lake.

As soon as the brief massacre was over, a Mexican colonel assigned soldiers to drive the remaining wagons to San Antonio. Several days later, when they had nearly reached their destination, an officer discovered the stolen silver bars were not among the goods in the wagon train. Assuming correctly that Trammel had hidden the silver in the lake, the soldiers went back to the area only to discover that recent rains had raised the lake level more than five feet, thus preventing a search for the ingots. The soldiers returned to San Antonio, and history records no further efforts on the part of the Mexican government to recover the treasure.

Dawson, the teamster who escaped the onslaught of Mexican soldiers, managed to make his way to St. Louis, where he reported the massacre and the hurried disposition of the six wagonloads of silver bars. Dawson made several attempts to organize a group to return to the lake and recover the treasure, but he was never able to secure adequate financial backing. Dawson died several months later from consumption, but up until his last living moments, he clung to the truth of the story of the huge fortune in silver in the small lake in the East Texas piney woods.

The hidden treasure of silver ingots, long settled into the soft and sandy depths of the lake bottom, was not forgotten. In 1895, three Mexicans carrying maps and descriptions of the terrain, arrived in the area to search for the treasure. Designating one portion of the body of water now called Hendricks Lake as the area into which the wagons would most likely have been rolled, they began to drain it. Their plan had promise until they found that underground water seepage filled the lake nearly as fast as the Mexicans could draw it off. After several fruitless weeks, the trio gave up and went home.

In the early 1800s, a settler named Fox Tatum, after whom a nearby town was named, heard the tale of the six wagonloads of treasure in the lake near his property. Tatum tried to drain the lake in 1855, but was unsuccessful.

Over the years, the story of the hidden Spanish silver entered the realm of legend, and serious attempts to recover the great treasure all but ended. Then, in 1928, three fishermen brought to the surface three bars of silver they found in shallow water not far from where they had launched their boat. They spent several days searching for more ingots, apparently in vain, and the exact location of their discovery has since been forgotten.

In 1959, a drilling company from Houston was sinking some exploratory wells in the area. As part of their operation, the company set off dynamite charges near the lake, causing a portion of it to be drained. During the days after the lowering of the lake level, a very old wagon wheel was found along with several pieces of wood that looked as though they could have been part of a freight wagon. The wheel was subsequently identified as being at least a hundred years old.

In the 1960s, a man using a powerful metal detector stated that one part of the lake gave off positive indications of the presence of a dense cluster of metal on the bottom, but no formal search was ever undertaken.

In 1975, two men with diving gear discovered several pieces of wood, metal fittings, and an iron rim from a large wooden wagon wheel. After three more days of diving, however, no evidence of silver was found, and the men packed up and went home.

Perhaps the divers gave up too soon. The bars of silver would have settled deep into the soft muck of the lake bottom, perhaps only a few inches below the scattered remains of the old freight wagons, where they remain today.

References

Anderson, Nina, and Bill Anderson. *Southern Treasures*. Chester, Connecticut: The Globe Pequot Press, 1987.

Atchley, D. Van. "Treasure near Wichita Falls." *Lost Treasure,* March, 1977.

Bartholemew, Ed. *Money in the Ground.* Fort Davis, Texas: Frontier Book Co., 1974.

Carson, Xanthus. "The $63 Million Inca Loot That Landed in West Texas, Part II." *Lost Treasure,* January, 1977.

_____. "The $63 Million Inca Loot That Landed in West Texas, Part I." "*Lost Treasure,* December, 1976.

Casey, Robert J. *The Texas Border.* New York Bobbs-Merrill Company, Inc., 1950.

Chrisman, Harry E. *Tales of the Western Heartland.* Athens, Ohio: Swallow Press/Ohio University Press, 1984.

Dobie, J. Frank. *Coronado's Children,* Austin, Texas: University of Texas Press, 1930.

_____. "The Pull of the Minometer." *Old West,* Fall, 1968.

_____. *Legends of Texas.* Dallas, Texas: Southern Methodist University Press. 1924.

Goodall-Adams, John H. "Lost Ledge of Pure Silver." *Lost Treasure,* January, 1978.

Hughes, Brent. "Singer's Treasure on Padre Island," *Lost Treasure,* February, 1988.

Jameson, W.C. "The Lost Goatherder's Treasure, Part II." *Lost Treasure,* April, 1991.

_______. "The Lost Goatherder's Treasure, Part I." *Lost Treasure,* March, 1991

_______. *Buried Treasures of the American Southwest.* Little Rock, Arkansas: August House, Inc., 1989.

_______. "Found: Old Ben Sublett's Mine." *Gold,* Winter, 1975.

_______. "The Lost Juniper Springs Treasure." *Treasure,* March, 1985.

_______. "The Sad Saga of Rolth Sublett, Treasure Hunter." *True West,* August, 1985.

Jordan, Terry G., Bean, John L., and Holmes, William M. *Texas.* Boulder, Colorado: Westview Press, 1984.

LeGaye, E.S. *Treasure Anthology.* Houston, Texas: Western Heritage Press, 1973.

Miles, Elton. *Tales of the Big Bend.* College Station, Texas: Texas A&M University Press, 1976.

Palmore, Frank E. "Gold Coins At Rock Crossing." *Lost Treasure,* August, 1987.

Penfield, Thomas. *Dig Here!* San Antonio, Texas: The Naylor Company, 1962.

Probert, Thomas. *Lost Mines and Buried Treasures of the West.* Los Angeles, California: University of California Press, 1977.

Roundtree, J.G. "Lost Silver Ledge." *Treasure World,* February-March, 1971.

Sems, Verne. "Mexican Bullion on the Flying H Bar Ranch." *True West,* July-August, 1966.

Townsend, Tom. *Texas Treasure Coast.* Austin, Texas: Eakin Press, 1979.